MATELOT,
LITTLE SAILOR OF BRITTANY

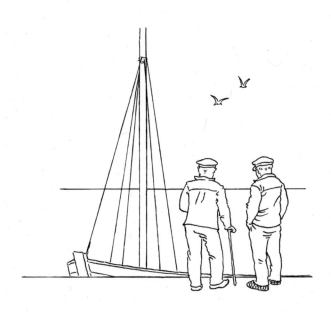

Books by Rosalie K. Fry

BANDY BOY'S TREASURE ISLAND
BUMBLEBUZZ
CINDERELLA'S MOUSE AND OTHER FAIRY TALES
LADYBUG! LADYBUG!
PIPKIN SEES THE WORLD
THE WIND CALL
A BELL FOR RINGELBLUME
MATELOT, LITTLE SAILOR OF BRITTANY

MATELOT,

Little Sailor of Brittany

Written and illustrated by
ROSALIE K. FRY

E. P. DUTTON & COMPANY, INC.
NEW YORK, 1958

Library of Congress Catalog Card Number: 58-12565
AMERICAN BOOK–STRATFORD PRESS, INC., NEW YORK

To Betsy

Chapter One

"Oh, can we go round to the harbor now at once, before we un-pack or anything?" begged Lucinda from the window where she stood watching the fishing boats coming in from the sea.

She soon discovered that her parents were every bit as impatient as she was—this was their first afternoon in Brittany and their first glimpse of the wild coast of Finistère, and they were just as eager as she was to get out and see it all. And so it was not long before the three of them were hurrying over the flowery strip of sand dune that was all that divided the beach from the cottage in which they were staying.

As they ran over the edge of the low dune they came upon a

surprisingly busy scene, for all along the shore the seaweed gatherers were at work; men bringing in shining loads in small flat-bottomed boats, while women stood at the water's edge, raking it into heaps. Another group tramped up and down the beach, carrying loads of weed to a waiting cart that stood on the sand with a patient horse dreaming between the shafts. The women seemed strangely dressed for such a job, in short black velvet dresses, and on their heads tall coifs of exquisite lace with long embroidered streamers flapping in the wind.

At any other time Lucinda would have been the first to stop and watch this fascinating scene, but now the fishing fleet was coming in and she felt she could not bear another boat to reach the harbor before she was there to see it arrive. So she led the way along the sandy track that ran round the edge of the bay, hurrying until her parents found it hard to keep pace with her. Nor did she stop when she came on a group of boatbuilders at work on a wooden ship, although she slackened her pace just long enough to shuffle her feet in the shavings and sniff the smell of the sawed wood which was even stronger than the tang of the seaweed at this point.

"Oh dear, there's so much to see!" she panted. "I do hope everything will wait till I have time to look at it carefully."

"Well this boat won't be moving away in a hurry anyway!" laughed Daddy, looking down on the graceful half-built hull taking shape on the beach below.

They hurried on again and at last they reached the harbor. The tide was high and the boats were drawn up all along the quay. And what colorful boats they were, their hulls and masts and wheelhouses painted brilliant green or blue, with perhaps a

8

touch of white or a line of scarlet here and there. From their colored masts heavy brown fishing nets hung drying in the sun, with bunches of green glass balls dangling among the folds. And the crews themselves added their own touch of color, some dressed in blue and others in red or russet brown, fading to every shade of rose and pink and orange. Between the boats the green harbor water glittered in the sunshine.

"All this marvelous color to paint!" exclaimed Mummy happily. "It's going to be hard to know where to begin."

Lucinda noticed that Daddy had already started scribbling details of rigging and fishing gear on the back of an envelope.

The quay was crowded; there were groups of white-coiffed women with baskets on their arms, waiting to buy fresh fish, and there were old sailors and brown-legged children who were simply there to see the boats come in; there were babies in arms and dogs and bicycles and the two-wheeled carts on which the crews pushed their catches away from the harbor.

Lucinda wandered along the line of boats trying to puzzle out their names, but some were French and some were Breton, and most of them too difficult to read.

And then she noticed a boy standing on the quayside eagerly watching a green boat coming in through the harbor entrance. He was older than she was, ten she guessed, or possibly even eleven, and he was quite unlike the dark-eyed children running about the harbor, for he was fair and freckled, and instead of their brief shorts and gay blue blouses he wore navy jeans and a T shirt.

"P'raps he's English or American," thought Lucinda hopefully, realizing that it might be fun to have someone of her own age to talk to sometime, although she was far too shy to approach him now. And then she forgot all about him as the green boat turned and headed in toward the quay where she was standing. As the boat came near with the white gulls wheeling about her and her emerald-green paintwork gleaming in the sunshine, Lucinda decided that she was the prettiest boat of them all. One of her crew stood ready in the bows with a rope which he presently flung to a man on the quayside who caught it and made it fast.

As the boat came alongside Lucinda saw the name *Saint Corentin* painted in white letters over the wheelhouse windows. This was an easier name than most and she liked it, repeating it over to herself and wondering who Saint Corentin might be.

And then she noticed something she hadn't seen on any other boat, a stiff little wooden figure standing in a painted frame in the panel below the central window. He seemed an odd choice for a fishing boat, for although he carried a fish in one hand he was dressed in a bishop's robes.

But now there were other things to look at as the crew crowded into the bows and prepared to unload their catch. The quayside watchers gathered round, and suddenly there was the freckled boy again, dragging one of the two-wheeled carts through the crowd toward the boat. Lucinda was very impressed. Then he called out something to one of the crew and she realized that he was speaking French.

So I'll never be able to talk to him after all, she thought regretfully. She stood watching as he maneuvered the cart close to the side of the boat as though he was really one of the crew.

Most of the fish were already packed in shallow wooden boxes and these were now handed down from the boat and stacked on the cart. Then followed baskets, also filled with fish.

One of the crew was a young boy of no more than fourteen, wearing a yellow oilskin apron over his faded pink clothes. He and the freckled boy chatted as they worked, laughing so much that Lucinda wished she could understand their language and share the fun. She was so absorbed that she had no idea that her parents were standing behind her until Daddy tweaked her hair.

"It looks as though we've come to a pretty exciting place, doesn't it?" he remarked.

A group of women crowded around the cart, examining the fish in the baskets and choosing what they wanted.

"Look—surely that's our own Madame le Roux from the cottage?" exclaimed Lucinda.

"So it is," said Daddy. "Choosing fresh fish for our supper I expect."

"Oh, just look at those children!" cried Mummy suddenly, pointing to three little boys of Lucinda's age who were sculling across the harbor in an ancient boat.

"Oh, they'll be all right," said Daddy calmly. "I imagine they swim like fish, and anyway they've probably been managing boats like that for years."

Certainly nothing could have looked more natural than the way in which the little oarsman stood with his legs wide-straddled, swaying from side to side as he worked his single oar over the stern of the boat.

"I wish I could go out in a boat like that!" breathed Lucinda, watching them enviously.

"Well you'd certainly have to learn to swim before I'd let you

11

go out with children of that age," said Mummy very firmly.

"And now I suppose we'd better be getting back to eat that fish that Madame has got for us," said Daddy.

"Oh, need we go just yet?" began Lucinda. "I did so want to see—" But she changed her mind when she saw that the crew of the *Saint Corentin* were themselves leaving the harbor, pushing their laden cart toward the village. Most of the crowd had already dispersed, the babies were gone and the dogs were gone, and now the last of the bicycles passed them with two enormous tunny fish strapped to the carrier.

"I shouldn't have thought it was easy to tie those slippery fish to a carrier!" remarked Mummy.

"And I shouldn't have thought it was easy to ride a bicycle wearing clogs!" laughed Daddy.

The men of the crowd had not gone farther than the street behind the harbor, where they stood about in groups.

"Whatever are they doing?" asked Lucinda, as one man after another ran forward to aim a heavy metal disk at a coin balanced on a pillar of wood a couple of inches high.

"Why it must be the *galoches*," said Daddy as they passed

group after group absorbed in this curious game. The shouts of the men and the clink of the disks on the road followed them as they left the village and made their way along the sandy track above the bay.

The seaweed gatherers were still at work, making the most of the last hour of daylight. But once again Lucinda hurried past them. For she was remembering that in her hurry to get to the harbor she had scarcely noticed the cottage in which they were staying, and now she was suddenly eager to see what it was like.

Chapter Two

The low-lying land behind the sand dunes was dotted with gray and white cottages, their doors and shutters painted green or blue. Most of them had a short hedge or a bit of wall on the western side to protect them from the sea winds.

"And, my word, they must need that shelter in the winter," remarked Daddy. "Just imagine the storms that must sweep in here from the sea!"

Beyond this shelter the cottage gardens stood open to the dunes without any sort of border line to divide their few flowers and vegetables from the soft, sand-colored grass.

"I wonder if they use paint left over from the boats for their doors and windows," said Lucinda. "They're exactly the same colors."

"I dare say they do," said Daddy. "After all everyone in these cottages is sure to have some relation in the fishing fleet."

"I'm glad our cottage has green shutters anyway," she said. "They're just the same color as the *Saint Corentin* and she's my favorite ship."

At one side of the cottage grew a stunted fig tree, shaped by the wind to a flat umbrella. Beneath it the ground was worn bare and hard, where generations of the le Roux family had sat in its shade summer after summer. As she walked up the shell-bordered path toward it Lucinda saw a pair of legs in navy-blue jeans swinging under the branches, and the next minute the freckled boy dropped to the ground in front of her.

"Hullo!" he said. "I saw you in the harbor."

"So you aren't a French boy after all!" she exclaimed in surprise.

"Of course not, I'm American," he replied. "Why did you think I was French?"

"Well, I heard you talking to the people on that boat and you sounded like a French boy."

"There now, Robin, that just shows how your French is improving—nobody ever took you for a French boy before!" exclaimed Madame appearing in the cottage doorway.

Robin said nothing, but anyone could see that he was pleased.

"Are you staying here too?" Mummy asked him, thinking how nice it would be for Lucinda to have a companion.

"Yes, he's staying here while his parents travel," said Madame. His father has business in Paris and Rome and Amsterdam, and they felt Robin would be happier here by the sea than wandering about in cities. You see I was nurse to Robin's mother when she was a little girl."

"Ah, so that's where you learned to speak English so well!" said Daddy.

"Yes, that's where I learned!" She smiled. "I spent three years in the States before I married, and happy years they were. And now I've taught my family to speak English too—the boys are good but my husband is naughty about it I'm afraid, he says Breton and French are good enough for him! But now I must go and get your supper. You must be hungry."

They had finished supper, and Madame was starting to clear the table when Lucinda looked up and noticed the picture on the wall. It wasn't very well painted, the hard blue sea being covered with waves that looked like cotton wool. But the green ship was unmistakable, for there was her name, *Saint Corentin*, in white across the wheelhouse.

"Oh, Daddy, look!" she exclaimed. "That's the boat we saw in the harbor!"

"*Saint Corentin*—my husband's ship," said Madame proudly, pausing in the doorway. "And my ship too, for I am her *marraine*."

"What does '*marraine*' mean?" asked Lucinda.

"It means 'godmother,' " answered Daddy. "But I don't quite understand what that has to do with a ship." And he looked enquiringly at Madame.

"Ah, it is one of our customs here in Brittany," she explained. "You see when a ship is launched she is properly christened by the priests. She has a godfather and a godmother, and there is a ceremony in the harbor for which the ship herself is decked with flags and flowers."

"What a beautiful sight it must be!" said Mummy.

17

"Yes," said Madame, "it is wonderful. And solemn too, for there comes a moment during the ceremony when the *marraine* throws a sheaf of flowers into the water in memory of sailors lost at sea—so many seamen have lost their lives off our dangerous coasts. But," she added with a smile, "if the day is fine and calm as it was when *Saint Corentin* was christened, then the ship puts to sea at the end of the ceremony, taking the priests and godparents and others out beyond the harbor for a trip, and that is something to remember all one's life. But wait—I have a photograph here of the christening if I can find it."

She rummaged through some papers in a drawer, and brought out a faded photograph. It showed the *Saint Corentin* drawn up to the quayside which was crowded with friends and relations. On the deck of the little ship herself, under a line of flags, a table had been set up as a temporary altar and in front of this stood the two priests in their robes. Around them were grouped the members of the crew and their families, the women all in their tall embroidered coifs.

"See, there is the godfather," said Madame, pointing to a young boy who stood near the priests with a candle in his hands. In the crowd on the quayside stood a tiny boy in a long white robe, holding the sheaf of flowers that would later be thrown into the sea.

"Oh, if only I could have been there to see it all!" sighed Lucinda. "And is she really your husband's very own ship?"

"She is," said Madame. "And here he comes. He must tell you about it himself—and you will have to use your English now, Michel, because the little girl doesn't speak French," she added with a smile as she gently pushed the big man into the room.

He greeted them all smilingly, shaking hands with each in turn. When he came to Lucinda she looked up eagerly.

"Is *Saint Corentin* really your own ship Mr.—er Captain—?" she began.

"Just call me 'Michel,' everybody does," said the big man smiling down at her. "Yes, *Saint Corentin* is my own ship now. She was built by my father and she has been a family ship ever since. I myself am her *patron* since my father's death, and in my crew I have my brother, my wife's brother and my sons—my youngest here has just joined as *mousse*," and he turned to welcome a boy who now came into the room behind him, the same boy who had stood on deck in the yellow apron. As he shook hands with them all his father went on:

"I called him Pierre after good Saint Pierre the fisherman, and now he has followed the calling as I hoped he would."

"Saint Pierre is French for Saint Peter you see," Mummy explained to Lucinda.

"And what about that little figure you've got, the one with the fish in his hand? Do tell us about him, please," said Lucinda.

"Ah, Saint Corentin!" smiled Michel. "The saint from whom our ship takes her name.

"Well, my father carved that figure at the time when the ship was built. He wasn't much hand at that sort of thing and it's a simple bit of work, but we wouldn't be without our saint on board for anything, would we, Pierre?"

"No indeed!" replied the boy emphatically.

"Who was Saint Corentin?" asked Daddy.

"And why does he carry a fish?" asked Lucinda.

19

"Ah now, that is a long story. I haven't the English to tell it properly. Come, Pierre, you will tell it better than I."

The boy looked confused at finding everyone's eyes upon him, but he soon forgot his shyness in the interest of his story.

"Well, Saint Corentin was a holy man," he began. "He lived in a hermit's cell in a forest on the spot where the city of Quimper stands today. Beside his cell was a pool, and in this pool lived a fish—a miraculous fish. Every day Corentin caught this fish and cut off as much of it as he needed for his dinner—"

"Oh, poor fish!" gasped Lucinda, her eyes wide with horror.

"Ah, but wait till you hear the rest of it!" said Robin.

"It was a miraculous fish, you see," explained Pierre. "And when Corentin threw it back into the pool it immediately grew whole again, ready for the Saint's next meal."

"Oh, that's all right then!" breathed Lucinda, sitting back thankfully on the arm of her father's chair while Pierre went on with the story.

"One day King Gradlon passed through the forest with his followers, and being hungry he stopped and asked the hermit for a meal. Saint Corentin was worried because he had to cut a larger piece than usual from his fish. But by a miracle it increased in the pan until there was enough to feed the king and all his followers."

"And when King Gradlon heard what had happened," went on Michel, taking up the story, "he asked the saint to tell him all about his God who could perform such miracles. And he was so impressed by what he heard that he himself became a Christian, and Saint Corentin baptized him in the forest pool."

"And after that," said Robin, "the King promised to build his

capital on that very spot, and to make Corentin himself his first bishop. And that's how the city of Quimper came to be built, with the cathedral of Saint Corentin standing in the middle of it.

"And I'll tell you something else," he added. "There's a statue of King Gradlon himself high up on the cathedral between the two great spires. I want to see that before I go back to the States, but I haven't been to Quimper yet."

Lucinda was still pondering the story she had heard.

"So that's why Saint Corentin is holding a fish," she mused. "He was a good person to choose for a fishing boat wasn't he?"

"He certainly was," said Mummy, "but now I'm afraid it's time for bed."

"Ah well, it's getting dark anyway," said Robin mysteriously, looking out of the window, "so you'll get a grand surprise when you open your bedroom door."

"What sort of surprise?" asked Lucinda apprehensively, not at all sure she would like the kind of surprise that happened in the dark.

"If I told you, it wouldn't be a surprise," he teased. "But it's something you'll like, I promise. Come on, I'll show you!" and he bounded ahead of her up the steep little stairs and threw open the bedroom door.

"W-w-whatever is it?" she gasped as a great beam of light swept slowly across the ceiling and then went out, leaving them in darkness.

"That's the lighthouse!" said Robin proudly. "One of the brightest in the whole world. Look, there it is again!" And once again the brilliant beam swept through the little room.

"Will it go on flashing all through the night?" she asked.

"Sure," answered Robin. "It's there to warn the ships at night and keep them off the rocks. They can see it thirty-five miles away on a clear night."

Later, as Mummy was tucking her into bed, Lucinda said thoughtfully, "Madame has rather a sad face hasn't she?"

"Yes," said Mummy, "she has. And it's not surprising when you remember that all her family is at sea—I'm sure I should have a sad face too if you and Daddy spent your lives in a fishing boat off this dangerous coast."

"What a good thing they've got the lighthouse there to warn them anyway," murmured Lucinda drowsily, closing her eyes as the beam of light moved across her pillow. Before it flashed again she was asleep.

22

Chapter Three

When Lucinda and her parents came downstairs next morning they found Robin sitting on the bottom step waiting for them.

"Can Lucinda come to the harbor with me this morning?" he asked.

"That boy just haunts the harbor!" laughed Madame as she passed with a jug of hot coffee.

Very soon they were all haunting the harbor. Mummy and Daddy painted there all day long, trying to catch it at all states of the tide. Daddy particularly loved to go out when the tide was low and sit on some dinghy stranded on the mud. From here he would sketch the larger boats as they stood in the shallow water supported on special struts that prevented them from heeling over as the tide receded.

Mummy delighted in drawing the groups of fishermen who stood about the harbor, wearing wooden *sabots* or carpet slippers on their feet, or even both together, for the slippers fitted inside the *sabots* like socks. She made sketches too of the seamen's children who were always sculling about the harbor in their fathers' boats.

As for Lucinda and Robin they spent their days on the quayside, watching the boats come and go and following all the activities of the little port. As long as the *Saint Corentin* was in harbor they hung about her, hoping to be given some small job to do, and it was a proud and important moment when they were sent on some errand by the *patron* or his crew. When the *Saint Corentin* was away there were other boats to watch, and Lucinda soon learned to say their names and recognize their crews. After that it wasn't long before she was able to distinguish the different types—the tunny boats and trawlers and the rest—until she became almost as quick as Robin himself at spotting them coming in from the sea.

"You're getting to be quite like a Breton girl," he said approvingly. And indeed she almost began to look like one as the sun and the strong sea winds burned her a deeper and deeper brown.

One evening, after they had been in Brittany several days, Daddy came in from the harbor with a suggestion.

"I got talking to an artist out there on the quay this afternoon," he said, "a very pleasant French chap named Jacques. He's touring around the country in his car. Tomorrow, if it's fine, he hopes to go to Audierne, and he's suggested taking as many of us as like to go along."

"Oh how kind of him!" exclaimed Mummy.

"And what about you children, would you like to go?" asked Daddy.

"I sure would!" cried Robin. "I've never been to Audierne."

As for Lucinda she was happy to go anywhere just as long as Robin was there too.

Next day was fine and sunny and they set off right after breakfast. It was a delightful drive and they saw many things to interest them on the way; women washing clothes in roadside pools and boiling them in huge three-legged cauldrons over roadside fires; simple granite crosses half-hidden in the wayside grass and strange prehistoric stones towering up in unexpected places; and once a beautiful Calvary with carved stone figures grouped about the Cross. They passed villages and pine woods and stretches of open moorland, and then the road dipped to a lonely stretch of river where a boy and girl were piling vegetables into a small black boat.

"That's rather a surprising sight," remarked Daddy, looking in vain for any sign of a dwelling. "I suppose they must have a farm or a cottage tucked away somewhere near, although upon my word they might just as well have popped up out of the ground by the look of them."

"It's certainly easy enough to believe such tales in a place like this," Mummy said, smiling, as the road wound up from the river and over the moors. "I suppose Brittany has her own particular fairies, the same as other countries?"

"She has indeed," said M. Jacques seriously.

"What sort of fairies?" asked Lucinda, leaning forward with interest.

"Well, now, I'm afraid I don't know as much about them as I should," admitted M. Jacques. "But I have heard of the Korrigans—horrible little hairy men who live in caverns along the shore from which they ride out on seaweed rafts, and when they are about, let the fisherfolk beware! And then of course there are the famous Mary Morgan, another dangerous group of sea-born fairies who lure fishermen to their doom upon the rocks."

"Aren't there any nice ones?" asked Lucinda.

"Yes, there is another group known as the Margot-la-fée, and I believe they are inclined to be friendly to mortals. But now just look at this lot—they certainly aren't fairies!" he exclaimed, slowing down to allow two cream-robed nuns to shepherd a party of small children across the road.

"Oh what a picture they make in their reds and blues with those old gray buildings behind them!" sighed Mummy regretfully. "If only there were time to stop and paint everything!"

"Just wait till you get to Audierne," smiled M. Jacques. "You'll find plenty of color there, I promise you. But first I want to take you to Saint-Tugen; it's only a couple of miles from Audierne."

"Saint Tugen—I've heard of him," said Robin. "Surely he's the patron saint of mad dogs?"

"He is," said M. Jacques. "And he is also the saint to whom one prays for relief from toothache. You will see his statue in the church, standing between a mad dog and a child with a swollen face."

The ancient church stood among trees in the middle of the

little village. Here they left the car. But before going into the church M. Jacques led them down a narrow lane to see Saint Tugen's well.

"Oh how perfectly charming!" exclaimed Mummy when she saw it, and it certainly would have been hard to imagine a prettier holy well. It was surrounded by stone slabs with a shallow round trough to one side. At the back a little stone shelter with a pointed roof stood over the water.

"Is that Saint Tugen in there on the shelf?" asked Lucinda, pointing to a little figure who stood peeping out at them from the shadows.

"Yes, that is the saint," replied M. Jacques.

The overflow from the well ran under the lane in which they stood and into a square stone washing place where several women were busy with their laundry. Lucinda watched fascinated as they spread their clothes on the stones and, having soaped them thoroughly, proceeded to scour them hard with scrubbing brushes, first on one side and then on the other. She decided she would try this method herself next time she washed her dolls' clothes.

Now M. Jacques led them into the church and there was the queer old figure of Saint Tugen between a red-cheeked boy with a swollen face and a fiercely snarling dog. From the saint's hand hung an enormous golden key on a sky-blue ribbon.

"The key is Saint Tugen's emblem," explained M. Jacques.

There were other ancient statues in the church and they wandered about studying them all. Suddenly Robin said in a hoarse, excited whisper, "Oh look, here's one of Saint Corentin!"

"And here's a gorgeous model ship!" shrilled Lucinda a moment later, far too excited even to whisper over her discovery.

"That was probably presented by some crew saved from shipwreck off this coast," said M. Jacques. "Very likely they prayed to Saint Tugen in their moment of danger, and then when they were saved they presented this model ship to his church as a thank offering."

"What a very nice idea," remarked Daddy, bending down to study the intricate rigging of the beautifully made little ship.

As they were leaving the church M. Jacques noticed some small lead keys on a table, each tied with a scrap of colored wool. They were priced twenty-five francs each and he bought two, one tied with red and one with yellow.

"Voilà!" he smiled, handing one to each of the children. "Saint Tugen's key to protect you from mad dogs! And now let us get on to Audierne."

Chapter Four

Audierne proved to be even more colorful than M. Jacques had promised, for it was market day and the quays were crowded with stalls of fish and fruit and gleaming kitchenware. The harbor itself was full of fishing boats, and beyond their blue and green and crimson masts the little town stood clustered about the harbor, the old houses crowding as close to the water as they could get, seeming to peer over one another's roofs as they climbed the wooded hillsides. Between the houses steep lanes and flights of steps twisted up from the quayside.

The three grownups could scarcely wait to get to work. They decided to have lunch early so as to leave a long free afternoon in which to paint.

"How about taking our picnic up there by the river?" suggested Daddy, pointing to a beautiful spot where pine trees grew on a steep bank above a wide green river that flowed under a bridge to the harbor.

It was a perfect spot for a picnic and they settled down under the trees. The ground was smooth, and slippery with pine needles, and the air sharp with the tang of the trees themselves. Lucinda breathed deeply and decided that this was one of the nicest smells in the world.

Directly below them the river had scooped out a curving bay where a number of derelict boats lay on their sides in all stages of decay. Some were still moored to the trees and rocks although it was evident they were already beyond repair.

"Sad to think they'll never sail again," said Mummy.

"They're interesting all the same," remarked Daddy. "There must be old types here that have gone out of use entirely."

Robin scarcely noticed what he ate as he sat staring down at the boats, trying to distinguish the types he knew and guess how some of the others must have looked in their prime.

"Oh look!" screamed Lucinda so suddenly that she made everyone jump. She pointed to a kingfisher as it flashed out of one of the old hulks and skimmed up the river like a bright blue jewel. He returned a few minutes later, going straight back to the boat from which he had come.

"I expect he always perches in there," said Daddy. "No doubt he finds it a good place from which to fish."

"So that's one boat that is still being used for fishing, in a way," mused Lucinda. "I wonder if he chose that special one because it's the same color as he is—only it's more like a shadow of his color really, it's so faded."

"Anyway it is one boat that still has a living heart," said M. Jacques, smiling at Lucinda.

When lunch was over Robin turned to Lucinda's parents.

"Could Lucinda and I stay here while you paint, do you think?" he begged. "I sure would like to walk round these old boats and really see how they were made."

Mummy hesitated, but it was Daddy who gave the answer.

"I don't see why you shouldn't," he said. "Don't stay too long, that's all. You've got a watch haven't you? So suppose you come and find us in about an hour and a half, we'll be somewhere in the harbor over there."

The two children hurried down to the beach. Some of the boats, including the kingfisher's hiding place, were well out in the river, but many others were high and dry and they walked round these in turn. Most of the paint had flaked away, but on one or two shadowy names could still be seen—Lucinda was able to pick out *Venus* and *Sainte Thérèse*.

But Robin was more interested in the boats themselves.

"Look, this one was a *sardinier*," he said. "And these two were trawlers, oh, and here's one that could surely be repaired—ah, if only I were rich I'd buy her and get her repaired and sail her out to sea."

"Would you take me too?" begged Lucinda.

But Robin did not reply. His head was already inside a gaping hole in the side of another boat.

There were several hulls that had rotted beyond all recognition, showing only the keel and a few odd ribs above the mud. After these it was pleasant to return to something more complete.

31

"Say! Here's one we could easily climb!" exclaimed Robin. "Let's get up and pretend we really are at sea!"

He scrambled up the side as he spoke and hauled Lucinda after him. The deck was still in good condition, and they made their way to the stern which stuck out over the water, giving them the feeling that they really were afloat.

"The tide's still coming in quite fast," observed Robin, pointing to a piece of wood as it floated by. "If you half shut your eyes and stare at the water hard enough you can almost get the feeling that we're moving."

Lucinda got the feeling quite easily, and she leaned on the rail, lost in a dream in which she and Robin were sailing their boat over a far green sea. Robin, however, soon tired of watching the river and flopped down on the deck where a couple of planks were missing. He lay on his face and peered down into the hole. At first he could distinguish nothing, but gradually, as his eyes became accustomed to the dark, he was able to make out one detail after another. He began to see how the ship-wrights of long ago had fitted the ship together plank by plank. An exciting rivery smell came up through the hole in the planking, and deep down there in the darkness he could hear the quiet lap of the water against the hull.

By this time Lucinda's dreams had carried her far and far away. She had forgotten Robin entirely, and was quite startled when he suddenly sprang to his feet with a horrified exclamation.

"Golly, Lucinda! Just look at the water!" he cried. "I'd forgotten all about it."

Lucinda looked and saw that the river had risen and now surrounded their wreck completely. They ran to the side but saw at once that the water was far too deep to allow them to get away. Robin looked at his watch.

"The tide won't even be high for another twenty minutes," he said in a worried voice, "which means we won't get back to the harbor for at least an hour, and we ought to be starting now. Do you think your father will be awfully angry?"

Lucinda nodded solemnly.

"I'm afraid he may be," she confessed.

Robin looked about, wondering if there might be someone on the riverbank who would row across and rescue them, but there was nobody in sight, indeed the only sign of life on the tranquil river was the busy kingfisher who flashed in and out of his own old boat nearby.

"If the tide gets any higher won't this boat float away?" asked Lucinda nervously, already fancying she could feel the deck stirring under her feet.

"Of course not!" said Robin scornfully. "All these boats have been here for years and years—we've got nothing to worry about except the time." And he glanced at his watch again. In half an hour Lucinda's parents would be looking for them in the harbor, and here they were surrounded by deep water and the tide still rising.

"I suppose we couldn't possibly swim across. . . ." he began.

Lucinda shook her head unhappily. "I couldn't," she said. Then something caught her eye coming down the river toward them.

"Look," she cried. "A boat!"

They hung over the rail and watched it hopefully.

"I'll call out when it gets close enough and ask if they'll take us off," said Robin.

They could see two people in the boat, one in the bow, and the other, a boy, sculling over the stern. There was something piled in the middle of the boat between them. Robin shouted out as they drew near, but they never so much as turned their heads.

"They aren't going to stop!" cried Lucinda, aghast.

Robin tried again, and this time the boy paused for a moment and looked toward them, then with a wide sweep of his oar turned and headed inshore.

They could now see that a girl sat in the bow, a dark wild-looking girl with a mop of black hair and a face tanned copper-brown. Both she and the boy had a vague, bewildered look about them as though their minds were far away.

"Why," exclaimed Lucinda suddenly, "they're those two we saw up the river, filling their boat with cabbages and things."

34

"Maybe that's why they don't seem to understand my French," said Robin. "Living way up there in the wilds I guess they speak nothing but Breton."

As long as it is only Breton and not some queer fairy language, thought Lucinda nervously, remembering the talk of Korrigans and the wicked Mary Morgan. She wished they hadn't called out for help, but it was too late to draw back now, for Robin had managed to make them understand at last.

"They seem to be going to Audierne themselves, so they'll take us right into the harbor," he said cheerfully, climbing down into a space the girl had cleared among the vegetables. Lucinda followed reluctantly, sitting down with a sudden bump on a net full of carrots as the boy and girl shoved the boat clear of the wreck and headed out into midstream. They were a strange, unsmiling pair, and as soon as they were on the move they seemed to forget their passengers entirely. Lucinda looked toward the bridge. It was comforting to know that Mummy and Daddy were on the other side of it.

A moment later the boat shot under the bridge and into the harbor.

35

Chapter Five

After the quiet river the harbor seemed full of noise and movement: shouts from the boats and the market echoed across the water where a tall-masted tunny boat edged in between the smaller craft moored along the quayside. Overhead a seagull circled on widespread wings filling the air with plaintive cries.

"Mee-oo, Mee-oo," mimicked Lucinda looking up. "He sounds just like a cat doesn't he, or anyway just like a kitten."

"Maybe that's why they call them sea mews," suggested Robin.

Their boat was halfway across the harbor when the girl gave a sudden gasp and stood up in her place in the bow, shading her eyes with her hand. Then pointing toward the harbor entrance she gabbled something in great agitation to her brother.

36

He swung round and looked where she pointed, then with a sharp exclamation threw all his weight against his oar until the boat slewed round and headed down the harbor toward the sea.

"Why are we going this way?" whispered Lucinda. "It looks as though we're going out to sea."

"I don't quite know," admitted Robin, and turning toward the boy he tried to make him understand that they wanted to be landed on the quay which was already slipping astern. But the boy paid no attention, and when Robin tried to make the sister understand she was no more interested than her brother, all her attention being concentrated on something that lay ahead.

Lucinda looked from one to the other. They were both very serious now, their black eyes intent and watchful, and suddenly she was really frightened. She looked back desperately toward the forest of masts in the harbor, knowing that Mummy and Daddy were somewhere there behind the boats. But she knew it was no use calling. They would never hear her voice above the harbor noises, nor would they notice this one small boat among so many others. She turned to Robin.

"Are they kidnaping us do you think?" she asked in a scared voice.

"Of course not!" retorted Robin who was secretly wondering the same thing himself.

Now they swept round a curve and the harbor was left astern, while ahead of them lay the open sea with one small coaster chugging out past the end of the sea wall ahead of them.

It now became clear that this coaster was what interested the brother and sister, and as she was traveling slowly they were able to gain on her inch by inch. As soon as they were near enough

37

the girl stood up again, and cupping her hands around her mouth gave a tremendous halloo.

They were close enough now to see a head pop up in the stern of the ship ahead, and a moment later an answering shout sounded across the water, followed by two sharp blasts from the ship's siren. More heads appeared on deck, and as they cleared the end of the sea wall the ship's engines slowed down until they were merely ticking over. There were shouts and laughter and a great deal of talk, but as this was all in Breton even Robin could not understand a word.

Then a rope was flung which the sister caught, making it fast to their own boat and gradually shortening it until they were close under the stern of the coaster. She was old and dirty and her rusty paint was black, a sad contrast to the blue and green boats to which Lucinda had become accustomed.

"I don't like it," she whispered fearfully to Robin. "Why are they towing us out to sea?"

"I don't know," he answered anxiously, trying to comfort himself with the thought that at least they were not going fast. Presently he spotted several small boats offshore, presumably fishing or laying lobster pots, and his spirits rose with the hope that they might pass near enough to get some help from one of these. Lucinda, however, had no such hopes, her attention having been caught by a strange bell buoy that moaned and grumbled to itself like some giant in agony.

Nobody paid any attention to Robin and Lucinda, being far too busy hoisting the vegetables on board, chattering all the while in Breton, while the evil-smelling engine sputtered fitfully. No one could possibly think of this as a fairy boat, but Lucinda had plenty of imagination, and it now turned in another direction.

"Oh Robin, suppose it's a pirate ship!" she quavered, looking up at the rusted hull.

To her astonishment a cheery voice replied, "Hullo! Hullo!—do I hear someone speaking English?" and a tousled head looked over the side—a head as wild as any pirate's except for a pair of twinkling eyes as blue as the sea itself. When the children saw that twinkle they felt better and ventured to tell this strange seaman their story. He roared with laughter when they came to the pirate part.

"Well I promise you we are neither kidnapers nor pirates," he assured them. "Although I admit we look like it in this old tub. It's a simple story really. We are on our way to the Ile de Sein and agreed to deliver a load of vegetables there for the skipper's cousin. But these kids were late bringing the stuff to the harbor and we couldn't wait any longer, and so they missed us—or very nearly missed us. But now you'd best be getting back before you are missed yourselves, especially as the tide has already turned."

The brother and sister were back in their places now, and the girl was busy untying the towline.

Robin had one last question to ask.

"Say—why are you on this boat anyway?" he demanded of their new friend. "You aren't a Breton are you?"

"Not I, I'm a Cornishman from England," he replied. "But I'd always heard that this part of Brittany is called 'La Cornouaille' because it is so like our own English Cornwall. So I took a job on a Breton ship so as to be able to come here and see for myself. And I'm not the first Cornishman to come across to

39

Brittany by any means—many of her early saints and holy men came to her from Cornwall—some of them even crossed the sea in boats made of stone."

"Stone?" echoed Robin unbelievingly.

"So they say," said the Cornishman, and suddenly there was that twinkle again. And so they guessed that although the saints and holy men were true enough the stone boats were probably part of a legend.

As soon as the children's boat was clear, the old ship's engines speeded up and she chugged out to sea. For a moment or two their own small boat tossed helplessly in the wash, but as soon as the worst of it died away, the boy gripped his oar and began to scull back toward the shore. But the tide was against them now and they moved slowly through the water, giving Lucinda and Robin plenty of time to look about them. Little by little the grumbling bell buoy slipped astern and they could soon see sandy bays along the coast under the low green cliffs. They had almost reached the harbor entrance when Lucinda noticed something floating in the water.

"What's that?" she asked.

"Only an old fish basket, plenty of those about," said Robin casually. "I expect it got left on one of the slipways and the high tide washed it off."

"It seems an awful waste," said Lucinda regretfully as the basket bobbed on its way toward the open sea. And suddenly as she spoke a small gray paw reached up over the rim of the basket and a piteous mew sounded over the water.

"It's a kitten!" she screamed. "Quick! Quick! We must rescue him before the basket sinks."

"What on earth do you mean?" asked Robin looking unbelievingly at the basket. "I don't see any kitten."

The gray paw had disappeared but Lucinda was certain she had seen it.

"I know it's there," she insisted. "Didn't you hear it cry?"

"Probably one of the sea mews," said Robin.

"It wasn't, it wasn't. I know it was a kitten," cried Lucinda desperately as the basket drifted farther and farther away.

Robin was persuaded against his will, but the dark boy was struggling to make headway against the tide and was in no mood to turn back for some *petit chat* that he hadn't even seen.

"Please, oh please!" implored Lucinda with a little sob in her voice, twisting her hands unhappily in her lap.

The strange dark girl could not understand her words but she understood the look on Lucinda's face, and she turned and spoke to her brother. After a short sharp argument he swung the boat about with an angry twist of his oar and headed away from the harbor once again. Robin took one look at his scowling face and muttered warningly, "There'd just better *be* a kitten, that's all!"

As they drew near the drifting basket Lucinda leaned over the side of the boat.

"We're coming to save you darling!" she called out encouragingly.

"No good speaking to a French cat in English!" scoffed Robin, hanging on to the back of her cardigan in case she fell overboard in her excitement.

It was the girl who managed to grab the basket with a boat hook, and it was Lucinda who lifted out the kitten. He was a miserable little object, all legs and eyes, with bedraggled gray fur and a white-tipped tail.

"He's terribly, terribly thin," she said as her fingers sank into his fur. She did not admit that he was also terribly fierce and had scratched her hand as she lifted him out of the basket. He struggled violently at first, but she held him firmly and presently he quieted down and mewed instead.

"There—that's what I heard!" she said triumphantly.

"He smells of fish," remarked Robin. "Maybe he got into that basket to look for something to eat." There were many such baskets on the harbor slipways and it was easy to see how this one could have been carried away by the tide.

"And if he was busy eating fish in the bottom he wouldn't have noticed it was floating until too late," he added.

"And if we hadn't rescued him he'd have been swept out to sea and never seen again!" said Lucinda with a shudder.

She stole a glance at the dark boy and noticed an amused half-smile on his face. The moment he saw her looking at him he set his jaw and scowled ahead as before, but Lucinda smiled to herself in secret, for she knew he was not as fierce as he pretended.

All the way back to the harbor the kitten mewed and mewed and mewed, and he was still wailing loudly when the boat drew in to one of the slipways. Lucinda and Robin scrambled ashore, then turned to thank their rescuers. But already the boat was moving off, and with no more than a brief nod and a half-smile the strange pair was gone. They crossed the harbor without once looking back and disappeared under the bridge.

"Well anyway," said Lucinda, "if they really did come up out of the ground like Daddy suggested they must have belonged to Margot-la-fée because they really were kind to humans this time weren't they?"

Chapter Six

Lucinda and Robin went in search of the grownups and they found Daddy almost immediately.

"What in the world have you got there?" he asked.

Together they started to explain, but the kitten's mewing interrupted every sentence.

"Here, let's get the poor creature something to eat before we try to do any talking," said Daddy. He led the way to a quayside café with its two red tables outside on the pavement. They sat at one of these and Daddy ordered a bottle of milk and a saucer for the kitten.

"And we might as well have something ourselves," he suggested. "What would you two like?"

"Please can I have *Pscttitt?*" asked Robin.

"Can you have *what?*" said Daddy.

"*Pscttitt!* That really is its name and it's scrumptious."

"And can I have it too?" put in Lucinda quickly.

"Certainly, have anything you like," smiled Daddy, "as long as I myself may stick to coffee!"

"I hope he knows how to drink out of a saucer," said Lucinda when the kitten's milk arrived. He knew all right! Indeed he knew so well that she had to refill his saucer three times before he was satisfied! After that he lay in her lap quite dazed and full and was very soon asleep. And now she was free to sample her *Pscttitt*. It was fizzy and tasted of orange. Robin was right, it was absolutely scrumptious. And then between them they started to tell their story again.

Just as they finished Mummy joined them and they had to tell it all over again for her. The part of the whole adventure that seemed to impress her most was the fact that they had been out in an open boat, and beyond the harbor at that.

"Only we didn't mean to," explained Lucinda earnestly, noticing Mummy's expression. "We wanted to come straight here, only they wouldn't turn back."

"Well, you're not to go out in any more boats until you have learned to swim," said Mummy very seriously. "Never, unless either Daddy or Mummy is with you. Is that quite clear?"

"Yes Mummy," answered Lucinda solemnly.

Now M. Jacques appeared and Daddy ordered another cup of coffee. When the girl brought it he asked her if she knew where the kitten belonged.

"Ah, *le petit chat*," she replied with a shrug, and went on to explain that the kitten was a stray, she had noticed him wandering about the harbor for days, picking up odd scraps of fish and mewing continually.

"A stray!" cried Lucinda joyously. "Then surely I can keep him and take home when we go?" She looked imploringly from one parent to the other.

45

"Oh darling child, I'm afraid we can't possibly take him home," said Mummy.

"You see he would have to go into quarantine as soon as we landed," Daddy explained. "And what's more he would have to stay there so long that by the time we got him back he'd be a grown-up cat and would have forgotten us completely."

"And anyway," said Mummy, "I'm sure a little French kitten would feel homesick among strange cats—why he wouldn't even understand their language."

"I hadn't thought about that," said Lucinda thoughtfully. "Well then, do you suppose Madame would give him a home as nobody seems to want him here?"

"I very much doubt she'll keep him herself as she has a cat already," answered Mummy. "But I dare say she'll be able to tell us of someone who'll give him a home. Anyway we can't very well leave the poor little creature here to starve."

The kitten opened his eyes with a drowsy mew and stretched in Lucinda's lap.

"My word, what claws!" exclaimed Daddy. "Is that where you got that scratch on your hand?"

"Oh, he didn't mean to do it," she said, and quickly changing the subject she went on, "we must think of a name for him, it ought to be something to do with the sea, since that's where we found him."

"Well in that case," observed Daddy with a private wink at Robin, "what about 'Sea Mew'—he came from the sea and does nothing but mew."

Robin collapsed with a shout of laughter, but Lucinda was not amused.

"Oh, Daddy, you're hopeless!" she scolded. "You know I don't mean that sort of name, I mean a proper one, something we can really call him."

Daddy tried again.

"Well then how about '*Matelot*'--that's the French for sailor, and he was certainly sailing when you found him."

This time Lucinda was delighted and Matelot became the kitten's name.

"I still like Sea Mew best," muttered Robin under his breath. But Lucinda pretended not to hear.

Matelot slept all the way home in the car and was still asleep when they got out at the other end.

They found the le Roux family sitting out under the fig tree, and once again the whole adventure had to be told while everyone admired the little hero of the story who lay asleep in Lucinda's arms.

She turned to Michel.

"Was it really true what the Cornishman told us?" she asked. "He said some of the saints came over here from England in boats made of stone. Surely they couldn't really, could they?"

"Well now, it's hard to say for certain," Michel answered seriously. "You see there have always been some who believed those tales to be true. And what is more, several of the stone boats—or parts of them—have actually been preserved in our chapels and churches. There is one near Auray—" Here he paused as though not quite sure how to continue.

"Do tell them," urged Pierre who knew what was coming.

"Well, you see," smiled Michel, glancing a little apologetically at Lucinda's parents, "you may find this hard to believe."

47

"Please do tell us," said Mummy persuasively. "I find there are so many things that are easier to believe in Brittany than anywhere else."

"Well then," said Michel, "in the chapel of Sainte Avoye near the town of Auray there is such a stone. It is said to be part of the boat in which Sainte Avoye herself crossed over the sea from Cornwall hundreds of years ago. Now this stone is supposed to have miraculous properties, and there were those who believed in olden times that if a delicate child was placed in Sainte Avoye's boat his health would improve. Now you may be surprised to hear, looking at me today, that I myself was a delicate child, indeed they never expected to rear me. But my great-grandmother insisted that she knew how to cure me, and one day she carried me off to the chapel of Sainte Avoye where she lifted me into the stone 'boat.' I was too young to remember the incident myself, but I have been told of it many a time. And certain it is that my health improved from that day, and the old lady always insisted that it was entirely due to Sainte Avoye's boat. So you see there are those of us who can never entirely disbelieve the tales of these old stone boats. And anyway," he finished simply, "is the thought of one person crossing the Channel in a stone boat so very much more wonderful, after all, than the thought of a thousand people crossing the wide Atlantic in a boat made of steel?"

"Especially when the stone boat was guided by a saint," said Mummy very softly.

At this moment Matelot opened his eyes and stirred in Lucinda's arms, and she remembered that a home had still to be found for him.

48

But Mummy had been right, Madame had no room for him herself.

"It wouldn't be fair on old Blanchette here," she said, stroking the large white cat that lay stretched in her lap. At the sound of her name Blanchette opened her eyes and the first thing she saw was Matelot. She uttered an ominous growling sound in her throat.

"You see what I mean?" said Madame.

Matelot did not wait for more. He struggled out of Lucinda's grasp, and using her arm and shoulder and head like the rungs of a ladder he sprang up into the fig tree where he crouched on the highest branch, spitting furiously.

"Don't worry," said Madame hastily, "we'll lock him safely into the shed tonight and in the morning I'll think of someone who may give him a home."

But Matelot must first be caught and this was by no means easy. Even when Blanchette had been shut away in the kitchen he refused to be coaxed from his perch. Finally Robin climbed up and brought him down.

"It seems to me," he said ruefully, licking a scratched and bleeding hand, "that we are going to need Saint Tugen's keys to protect us from a mad kitten rather than a mad dog."

Chapter Seven

Matelot woke them all with his plaintive cries next morning. Lucinda flew down to comfort him, but Madame was there before her with a saucer of milk.

"Shut the door," she cautioned. "We don't want Blanchette in here just now."

But the door was no sooner shut than it opened again and there stood Robin in his pajamas.

"I thought I heard something going on," he said, coming in to join them. The kitten crouched over the saucer lapping steadily.

"You can almost see him swelling," observed Robin.

"Have you thought of a home for him yet?" asked Lucinda looking hopefully up at Madame.

"As a matter of fact I have," she answered. "My cousin Yves called in last night after you two were in bed to ask if I would like a trip to Saint-Herbot, as he has business there this afternoon."

"Is Saint-Herbot a place or a person?" asked Lucinda.

"Both," explained Madame. "It's a village named after a saint who lived there long ago. My eldest sister's home is there, and as it is a long way off and nowhere near our bus route I seldom get a chance to visit her."

"Is that where you're taking Matelot?" asked Lucinda, watching the kitten's white-tipped tail twitching as he drank.

"Yes," said Madame. "I thought it might be a good place to try. Marie has a biggish place, she runs a little shop and a crêperie, while her husband's old parents have a small farm on the hillside. Marie has no cat that I remember, so it seems to me that either she herself or the old folk on the farm might well have room for a kitten."

"How are you going to get there if there isn't a bus?" asked Robin.

"Oh, Yves has a truck," replied Madame.

Robin drew a deep breath.

"Could I go with you?" he begged. "I've never been in a truck."

"Why yes, of course, if you'd like to," smiled Madame. "There's plenty of room on the front seat."

"I've never been in a truck either," murmured Lucinda. "I suppose I couldn't go too?"

"Well, you'd have to ask your parents first, but you can certainly come if they agree. I can't say what time we'll be back, but I dare say your mummy won't mind if you're a bit late for once."

Mummy and Daddy were delighted to have Lucinda go once Madame had assured them that she wouldn't be in the way. Yves was not calling for them until after lunch so there was time to go to the harbor as usual first. Just as they were starting out Madame called Robin back and handed him a basket.

"See what they've brought in in the way of fish this morning," she said, "or crabs or lobsters—anything that looks nice. Tell the men you want something to take to the folks in Saint-Herbot and get whatever they advise. Fresh fish is always a treat in the inland villages."

"Inland?" echoed Lucinda in dismay. "Isn't Saint-Herbot by the sea?"

"No, dear, it's right inland, but surely you won't mind leaving the sea for an afternoon?"

"Oh it's not for myself, it's for Matelot," explained Lucinda. "You see he's a sailor kitten, he came from the sea and I'm so afraid he mightn't be happy away from it."

"Oh, come now," said Daddy firmly. "It's no good having fancy ideas about Matelot. He's mighty lucky to have the chance of a home at all."

After a lunchtime saucer of milk Matelot was put into a basket with a cloth tied over the top to prevent his escaping. He started to mew immediately and Lucinda could feel him threshing about as she carried the basket out to the roadside where they were meeting Yves.

The truck was there already and Yves came forward to meet

53

them with a smile. He could not speak a word of English but Lucinda thought his friendly grin as good as any "Hello." He dumped the basket of fish in the back of the truck, but she decided that Matelot would be happier if she held his basket on her lap.

Yves opened the door of the driver's cab and they all scrambled in. Robin sat next to Yves so that he could watch him shifting gear and secretly pretend to be driving the truck himself. Lucinda sat next to him with the basket on her knee and Madame sat beyond.

They slammed the door, then Yves revved up the engine with a roar and they started off. The truck was old, and what with the noise of the engine and the clatter and clank of the loosely bolted woodwork it was difficult to do much talking and impossible to hear whether Matelot was crying or not. But as his basket no longer thumped and heaved Lucinda hoped he had dropped asleep and gave herself up to the enjoyment of the journey. The high seat of the truck proved a wonderful place from which to see everything. She found she was able to look over gates and garden walls and see the countryside that lay beyond the hedges.

Robin kept his eyes on the road as a driver should, sounding an imaginary horn in his head and trying to guess when Yves was going to swing out and pass, or wave the traffic on.

At first their road followed the coast over stretches of marsh and moorland, and through scattered fishing villages where nets lay spread out to dry on the whitewashed walls. Then as the road turned away from the sea the villages grew into little towns, and the marsh gave place to orchards where drowsy cows lay chewing their cuds, tethered by ropes and chains fastened to their horns. Farther inland there were woods and rivers, and sheltered cottages bright with roses and morning glory. Then the road climbed to a moorland ridge where pine trees stood on a hillside blazing with the gold and purple of gorse and heather. As they drove along this upland road Lucinda looked far out over the country in all directions but nowhere could she catch even a glimpse of the sea.

"Oh I do hope he won't miss it," she whispered, as her arms tightened unconsciously about the kitten's basket.

Robin pointed suddenly to a milestone in the grass.

"Saint-Herbot 1 kilometre," he read.

The road was dipping steeply now, but it was impossible to see beyond the first bend, for the trees crowded down the hillside as though anxious to hide what lay below. But at last a turn of the road brought the village into view, lying among the greenest fields Lucinda had ever seen. Along the roadside a line of snow-white sheets blew out on the summer wind, and everywhere was the sound of running water.

Surely even a sailor would love this place, she thought as she climbed down from the lorry, clutching the kitten's basket. Yves handed the basket of fish to Robin, then drove away, promising to call for them as soon as his job was done. Madame and the children turned down the road where the white sheets were blowing.

In the middle of the village rose the tower of a beautiful chapel, and an old man was leading a lame black cow over the field toward it.

55

"He must be taking her to Saint-Herbot," remarked Madame. "She's very lame I see."

"Why does he take her to Saint-Herbot?" asked Robin.

"The good Saint-Herbot is the patron saint of horned cattle in this part of Brittany," explained Madame. "His help is always asked for cattle that are sick. Inside the chapel itself there are two stone tables on which the farmers place hairs from the tails of their cows as offerings to the saint."

"Will he give hairs from that cow's tail?" asked Lucinda, watching the bent old man who hobbled along almost as painfully as the cow herself.

"He will indeed—but look who's here. Ah, Marie! Marie!" and she ran with outstretched hands toward a woman who was kneeling by the roadside, washing clothes in one of the sparkling streams that trickled down from the hill.

Marie was short and fat, but she scrambled to her feet in a breathless hurry and flung her arms around Madame, giving her three tremendous kisses, after which she turned and shook hands with the children. Then, leaving her washing where it lay on the roadside stones, she led them toward her house which had the word "Crêperie" painted over the door. The children would have liked to stop and look at the picture post cards in the cluttered little shop, but she hustled them through into the room beyond, talking so hard that it was impossible for anyone else to get in a single word.

"I should think we'd better leave the baskets here by the door," suggested Robin, dumping the basket of fish against the wall. Lucinda put her smaller one beside it.

"I think Matelot must be asleep," she whispered. "Anyway, he's quiet."

Marie signed to them all to sit round the table and hurriedly fetched out plates, chattering all the while.

"Oh goody, she's going to give us crêpes," whispered Robin.

"What are crêpes?" asked Lucinda.

"Like pancakes, only much, much nicer—they're as thin as sheets of paper and all crunchy round the edges. You just wait, they're marvelous."

The two women talked unceasingly, their voices growing more and more excited. Lucinda watched them anxiously, fearing that such head-shakings and waving of hands could only mean that Marie had no room for Matelot after all.

"Can't she take him, Madame?" she asked in a worried voice as soon as there was a pause in the conversation.

"Take who?" asked Madame, very puzzled.

"Matelot," said Lucinda.

"Why we haven't even mentioned him yet," said Madame. "You see Marie and I haven't met for a while and I've all the family news to tell her."

Lucinda was astonished. She hadn't supposed that anything as important as Matelot had happened in the family lately. The conversation went on again and she leaned back in her chair and looked about the cheerful little room.

Against one wall was a carved wooden dresser, studded all over with bright brass-headed nails arranged in patterns, and built into the center of this dresser was a wonderful grandfather clock. A wreath of flowers was painted around its face, and in place of the usual pendulum an enormous sheaf of golden corn decorated with poppies and purple grapes, swung backwards and forwards behind a glass-paneled door. On either side of the clock bright pottery plates stood on the dresser shelves, only instead of leaning back against the wall they all tipped forward against a wooden rail which Lucinda thought a very strange idea. On the mantelpiece was a row of canisters. She began to spell out the words on them to herself; *café* of course was coffee, and *sucre* she knew was sugar, and after a moment's thought she remembered that *thé* was tea.

But now Robin was nudging her.

"Watch now, she's going to make the *crêpes*," he whispered.

As he spoke Marie poured some thin batter out of a bowl on to a hot griddle on the stove, smoothing it out to the edges as though spreading butter on a slice of bread. It soon began to grow crisp and brown, and immediately Marie caught up the edge and deftly flipped the whole thing over to brown on the other side. Then folding it in half she hurried across and put it on Lucinda's plate.

"*Voilà!*" she cried with a beaming smile, then hurried back to the stove to make the next one. Now for a while she actually forgot to talk at all as she made one *crêpe* after another, piling them on to the three plates as fast as they could eat them.

"You're quite right," agreed Lucinda. "They're a million times nicer than pancakes."

Eventually they reached the stage when they had eaten all they could manage, although by no means all that Marie was prepared to make.

And now at last they came to the subject of Matelot.

It seemed that Marie was willing to take him although it couldn't be said that she sounded particularly interested.

"Shall I go and get him?" suggested Lucinda hopefully.

As soon as she picked up the basket the kitten started to mew and the instant she removed the cloth he flew out like a jack-in-the-box.

"Um . . ." muttered Marie. However she poured some milk into a saucer and put it on the floor. But the kitten wasn't interested, he was far too restless, prowling about the strange room and examining the dark places under the furniture, ready to jump aside and spit at every sound.

"I think you two had better leave him to get used to his new surroundings in his own way," suggested Madame. "You can go out and explore if you like. Yves won't be ready for a while. Now mind the kitten and be sure to shut the door as you go out."

59

"Let's go and look at the cow's hair in the chapel," suggested Robin.

In the churchyard they met the old man and his cow. She was still limping painfully, but no doubt even Saint-Herbot would take a day or two to work the cure. Lucinda thought that both the cow and her old master had a peaceful look about them as though they knew that their prayer would be answered soon.

Robin asked the old man about the cow, but he shuffled by without a word and they realized he was deaf. The cow, however, paid them more attention, for when Lucinda stroked her nose she rolled long-lashed eyes and gave her a friendly look as she limped by. The children stood in the gateway and watched the strange pair amble off, the large black cow and the little old man who was all black too, wearing a black velvet waistcoat under his suit, and a velvet hat that had once been black with a bunch of long black ribbons fluttering out behind. Even his wooden *sabots* were painted shiny black, and they were stuffed with straw which sprouted up around his thin ankles in place of socks.

"Now let's go inside and see if he's left any hair," said Robin.

The chapel was dim and cool after the brilliant sunshine, but they saw the stone tables immediately, and on one was a little heap of coarse black hair.

"So it must be hers," said Lucinda.

They wandered about the chapel, looking at the ancient effigies. There was a kind-faced one of Saint-Herbot, and one of Saint Yves, and even one of Saint Corentin although without his fish.

"Would our Yves from the truck have been named after this

Saint Yves, do you suppose?" asked Lucinda, looking up at the old statue.

"Sure to have been," replied Robin. "But now come on, let's go out into the sun."

Lucinda wished she had something to put into the old, old collection box in the porch, but as usual her pockets were empty.

After the silence of the chapel they noticed the sound of the wind in the churchyard trees and the trickle of running water. And Robin was sure he heard the hum of bees.

"And there they are!" he cried. "Up there round the top of that window, they must have a nest in the chapel."

But Lucinda was looking up at an old stone figure standing in a niche over one of the beautiful porches.

"He surely must be Saint-Herbot!" she mused. "What a gentle face he has, he looks like a person who would be kind to animals." And she smiled up at the simple little figure, worn smooth by centuries of wind and rain.

They wandered into the village street and there they found Madame and Marie sitting outside the créperie in the sun.

"So you've been into the old chapel," smiled Madame. "Did you see Saint-Herbot?"

"Yes, and the hair from that lame cow's tail—but, Madame, why is Saint-Herbot the patron saint of cattle?"

"Well, the tale goes that a farmer lent him a pair of white oxen to plow his land. But these two beasts became so fond of the saint that they entirely refused to leave him, and were always to be found after nightfall, asleep in the chapel porch. And from there any farmer who wished might borrow them, provided he returned them to Saint-Herbot before dawn.

61

"And after that, on the day of Saint-Herbot's *Pardon* in June, all the cattle in the district are supposed to rest from work."

"Oh how nice for them!" said Lucinda. "He looks that kind of a saint."

"As a matter of fact he came over here from Britain—perhaps that's why he was so 'specially fond of animals."

But now Yves rattled up in his truck and it was time to say good-by and go. Lucinda slipped indoors to say good-by to Matelot, but he was nowhere to be found.

"Far better leave him undisturbed," advised Madame. "He calmed down and drank his milk after you'd gone out, and now he's probably busy exploring his new home."

Yves had already started the engine when he remembered the baskets. He ran indoors and fetched them and shoved them into the back of the truck, then jumped up into his seat beside Robin and they started off.

Lucinda missed the heavy little basket on her knee, but she hoped that perhaps the kind Saint-Herbot might find time to watch over a homesick kitten as well as the local cattle.

At last they were home and Yves drew up with a jerk and stopped the engine. Immediately everyone was startled by a loud "Miaou!" They looked at one another in astonishment, then Yves jumped down and dragged the baskets out of the back. As he dumped them on the ground a small gray shape shot out of the fish basket.

"Matelot!" gasped Lucinda.

Yves and Robin collapsed with roars of laughter in which they were joined by Michel and Pierre who had come out to the road to meet them. But Lucinda was looking apprehensively at

Madame who had picked up the kitten and was staring at him as though she could scarcely believe he was real. He twitched his tail and mewed again and suddenly she laughed too.

"Never mind," she said. "We must find him another home, that's all."

"You know I'm beginning to think Lucinda's right about the sea," remarked Robin. "I bet he hid in that basket because it smelled of the sea."

"That's what comes of calling a kitten 'Matelot,'" laughed Michel.

Chapter Eight

Matelot woke them all again next morning. When Lucinda went down she found Madame all ready with plans for another home.

"It's a farm this time," she said. "There's always room for another cat on a farm. And it's not far off so he should be happy shouldn't he?" and she smiled understandingly at Lucinda.

So once again Matelot was packed into his basket and the cloth tied firmly over the top in spite of his angry protests. Then Madame explained carefully to Robin which way they must go, and he and Lucinda set off across the sand dunes carrying the basket between them.

They passed numbers of gray and white cottages just like their own, some with sky-blue shutters and some with green. The shutter holders were all alike in the shape of tiny people in round flat hats. Fishermen's jackets and trousers flapped on many clotheslines, while on others there were newly washed carpet slippers pinned in dripping rows. *Sabots* stood in the doorways, often stuffed with straw. Between the cottages wild flowers grew in the soft yellow grass of the dunes.

"Oh good!" exclaimed Lucinda. "It's going to be fine—the poor man's weather glass says so."

"What are you talking about?" asked Robin.

"Don't you know about scarlet pimpernel?" asked Lucinda in surprise.

Robin shook his head.

"Never heard of it," he said. "What is it?"

Lucinda picked one of the tiny scarlet flowers for him to see.

"There!" she said. "When it's open like that it means fine weather, and when it's shut it means bad."

"But does it really work?" asked Robin unbelievingly.

"Of course it does, that's why it's called 'poor man's weather glass.' "

A moment later Lucinda stopped again.

"Oh look at these, what can they be?" she exclaimed, stooping to stroke a tuft of biscuit-colored fluff that nodded on a thread-like stem. "Oh feel it, it's as soft as the top of Matelot's tail—and the same shape too. I know! I'll call it kitten grass. I've heard of cotton grass so this can just as well be kitten grass."

Robin, however, had more important things to think about, for he was busy concentrating on Madame's directions.

"I think this must be the track she meant," he murmured. "There are two cottages like she said, and some trees, oh, and there's the road so it must be right, come on, that must be the farm over there."

As they drew near they saw that it was a large farm with high gray walls. Lucinda paused and looked back.

"You can still see the sea from here," she remarked happily, "and I can even smell the seaweed, can't you?"

"Yes I can," answered Robin. "Well, in that case he ought to be all right here. Now we must find the way in."

They skirted the farm buildings looking for the entrance. Presently they came to a low wall. Lucinda looked over and saw an extraordinary sight; five little straw houses in a row, all with rounded woven walls and steep straw roofs with overhanging eaves. She clutched Robin's arm.

"Look!" she whispered. "Who lives in those? They look like goblins' houses."

"Pooh! They're only beehives," scoffed Robin. "If Matelot is silly enough to meddle with them it will be his own lookout."

They rounded a corner and came in sight of the farm entrance. An archway led through a tremendous wall into a farmyard. A whitewashed farmhouse stood to one side, the other two sides being enclosed by haystacks. Under one of these was a square cave-like opening with heavy wooden beams to hold back the hay at the sides and over the roof. A farm cart had been backed into this strange little shelter, and on it a number of hens were roosting.

Before they had time to knock at the door the farmer's wife came out into the yard followed by two shy little girls. Robin explained where they came from, and, when the woman smiled and nodded on hearing Madame's name, he went on to tell the story of Matelot's rescue from the sea. Lucinda couldn't understand a word, but she knew from his excited tones that that must be what he was talking about. She unfastened the cloth and Matelot's head popped out.

66

"Ah—*le petit chat de la mer*," laughed the woman.

"Little cat of the sea—that's just exactly what he is," said Robin lifting him out of the basket.

"Tell them his name is Matelot," said Lucinda.

But before there was time to say anything more their attention was caught by the smaller girl who was backing away with a frightened look on her face, whispering something softly under her breath. Her mother laughed, and taking the kitten from Robin she handed it to the older child. The little one mumbled something else and scuttled out of the farmyard as fast as her fat little legs would carry her. Her mother and sister laughed again, then Robin picked up the empty basket and turned to go.

"Good-by, darling," murmured Lucinda, reaching out to give the kitten one last pat before running out under the archway after Robin. At the bend of the path she looked back, and the last she saw of Matelot was his small gray head against the child's red jersey.

"He surely ought to like it there," she said. "Anyway it's so close we can easily come and visit him. But what did that little girl say, and why did she run away—surely she couldn't be scared of Matelot?"

"Her mother called him a little cat of the sea, it was that that scared her," answered Robin.

"But why?" asked Lucinda, very puzzled.

"Well you see she was afraid a cat of the sea must have come from the City of Ys—the drowned city that lies beneath the waves—and she was scared that the wicked Ahès herself might come to the farm to search for him."

67

"But look, there she is!" interrupted Lucinda. The small girl was cowering against the wall beside the beehives.

"Poor silly kid," exclaimed Robin, and leaning over the wall he called out something reassuring. But the child merely shook her head and turned away.

"Oh well, if she thinks the bees are safer than Matelot I can't help her," said Robin with a shrug. "And all because of a silly old legend!"

Lucinda stood still for a moment to see what the child would do and was relieved when her mother came out and took her by the hand.

"So she'll be all right now," she said with a sigh of relief as she hurried after Robin.

"Do tell me about the City of Ys," she begged as soon as she caught up with him.

"All right. Well, there used to be a city called Ys on the coast not far from here, so the story goes, and its ruler was King Gradlon—you remember he was the one Saint Corentin fed with the miraculous fish, and it was he who made Saint Corentin Bishop of Quimper.

"Well, King Gradlon had a beautiful daughter named Ahès. But unfortunately she was also very wicked, so wicked that in the end she made the people of Ys as bad as herself. One day in a fit of wildness she opened the great dike that protected them from the sea. The water rushed in and flooded the whole city and everyone was drowned except the good King Gradlon who managed to escape to safety on his horse. He tried to save his daughter, but she was swept away and turned into a mermaid. And they say she still haunts the dangerous reefs surrounding her old home, fishermen declare they have heard her singing out there at night. There's an old man in the harbor who says he's sailed over the city many a time, and seen the drowned church spires among the seaweed down below, and even heard the bells of the city ringing under the water."

Lucinda's mind was so full of the city under the sea that she was scarcely surprised to look up and see what appeared to be a vivid blue lake in the sand dunes right ahead. And yet it hadn't been there when they passed the spot this morning she was sure.

"Look, Robin," she said, pointing it out. "Is that a lake?"

"Of course not! It's a fishing net, one of the blue sardine nets they use here, and a new one too by the color of it. They must be going to mend it. Come on, let's go down and look at it."

The huge net lay spread on the ground, its delicate mesh lying unevenly over the tussocky grass and clumps of flowers which poked through the holes in places. Not far off lay a second net, a brown one of heavier mesh, and on this three women were already at work, sitting down wherever they found a tear and setting to work to repair it right away. The children moved over to watch.

"This one looks just like a patch of heather," remarked Lucinda, and she was right. The net was an old one, faded in places to pink and even purple, and the colors stood out against the grass like a heathery strip of moorland. Along one edge lay a fringe of circular corks.

They're bringing some more now," observed Robin, hurrying

69

to meet a party of fishermen dragging a heavily laden fish cart across the dunes. But in place of the usual load of fish this cart was piled with fishing nets which they now unrolled, spreading them out on the grass.

They passed several more nets as they dawdled home, and they stopped to examine every one, looking for tears and counting the corks and watching the women at work.

When they got near the cottage Daddy came to meet them.

"M. Jacques has been round again," he told them, "and he's taking us out in the car again this afternoon."

"Where to?" asked Robin.

"Well first we're going for a swim—"

"Oh, boy!" interrupted Robin joyously.

"And then we're going to Notre Dame de Tronoën to see the oldest Calvary in Brittany. But come along now, we are having our lunch early. Madame has it ready and waiting."

71

Chapter Nine

M. Jacques dropped them near the beach and drove off, promising to meet them later by the Calvary. The children raced ahead with their bathing things.

"Don't go into the water until we come," Mummy called after them.

The sandy bay was white and dazzling and the sea so clear that they could see shells and pebbles scattered over the sandy bottom beneath the little waves. As soon as they were in their bathing suits they went out and sat on the sands.

"What sparkly sand it is," said Lucinda. "Look—my foot's all covered with fairy diamonds!"

But Robin was busily occupied in putting on a magnificent pair of red rubber frog feet. Lucinda looked at them longingly. Daddy had said she must learn to swim before she could hope for such things herself, and it began to look as though she would never learn. It wasn't that she was afraid, she wasn't a bit, it was just—well it was just that she didn't want to get out of her depth by mistake. And how could she be sure about that if she didn't keep feeling for the bottom just to make certain it was still there?

"I suppose you can swim?" she asked casually.

"Oh yes, can't you?"

"Well I awfully nearly can," she replied.

"And you awfully nearly could last summer," reminded Daddy, coming down from the dunes to join them. "It's that one foot that is always the trouble. You see," he explained to Robin, "once she's in the water Lucinda is just like a ballet dancer, always balanced on one toe!"

"Well it's hardly touching the ground at all," she insisted.

"That's what the ballet dancers like to think!" laughed Daddy.

"Well, I do try to swim!" she sighed.

"Of course you do," said Mummy coming up behind her. "Come along, let's go in and try again now."

There was a lovely tingle in the sea.

"Sort of chilly—only it doesn't make you cold at all," said Robin trying to describe the feeling.

"No, it certainly isn't cold," said Mummy, "just wonderfully invigorating. I think it's the nicest sea I've ever been in."

"So do I!" said Lucinda.

73

"Well, come on then, see if you can't swim in it," urged Daddy.

Lucinda floundered forward, trying valiantly, but the water was clear and they could all see that one toe on the sandy bottom.

Robin had goggles as well as frog feet, and he now put these on and dived under water. Lucinda hastily put both feet on the bottom and stood up to watch him. He soon came up spluttering and shaking his head.

"Lovely!" he gasped when he got his breath. "You can see everything down below." And he prepared to dive again.

"Now I'm going to dive down to the sunken city of Ys," he told Lucinda with a grin. "I'll see if I can bring you back a jewel from the royal treasure chest!"

Down he went and Lucinda watched him glide along the bottom. Presently he came up with something in his hand.

"There!" he smiled, handing her a strip of bright green seaweed. "Emeralds from the City of Ys!"

"Perhaps it was a bracelet that belonged to the Princess Ahès," suggested Mummy. "Come here, I'll fix it for you."

"P'raps it will bring me luck," said Lucinda hopefully, looking down at the twist of green round her wrist.

"Perhaps it will," said Mummy. "I believe emeralds are supposed to give protection from the perils of the sea."

Robin was diving again and Lucinda returned to her swimming attempts, while her parents swam just beyond in the deeper water.

It was Robin who saw Lucinda's foot leave the bottom and kick out behind like a swimmer's. He struggled back to the surface in a hurry to see if this could be true. And there she was, her face crimson with excitement and wet with the flying spray thrown up by her hands as she floundered along, really swimming at last! Robin flung himself through the water toward her.

"Good . . . wonderful!" he encouraged, and began counting her strokes out loud. "Eight, nine, ten . . . good, go on . . . twelve, thirteen . . . oh, wonderful . . . fifteen, sixteen . . . you needn't go so fast you know . . . eighteen, nineteen, twenty . . . oh, you're terrific, you can *really* swim now!" He beamed as Lucinda's feet sank to the bottom and she stood up gasping for breath.

They shouted the news to Mummy and Daddy who came hurrying to see for themselves. Lucinda felt suddenly anxious. Suppose I can't do it again? she thought. But she no sooner pushed off than she found she could do it perfectly easily, so easily indeed that she couldn't understand why she hadn't done it long ago.

"So I've lost my ballet dancer!" laughed Daddy. "Never mind, I like my mermaid even better!" and he caught her up in his arms and kissed her.

"Oh—and I've lost my bracelet!" she exclaimed.

"Ah well," said Mummy, "maybe Ahès took it back again in return for the gift of swimming which she gave you."

"Well it brought me good luck while I had it anyway!" said Lucinda happily, plunging forward to swim again.

It was a good thing the sea wasn't cold that day, because nobody wanted to leave the water on such an exciting morning. Lucinda swam and swam until she had no breath left.

75

"Now I'm afraid you really must come in," said Mummy at last.

"Well, anyway, I can swim back can't I?" called Lucinda letting the waves carry her in toward the shore.

"It's so easy," she said in a bewildered tone as they walked up the beach. "Why couldn't I do it before?"

"Perhaps because you needed an emerald bracelet to protect you from the perils of the sea!" said Mummy with a smile.

When they were dressed Daddy produced a huge slab of chocolate from his pocket, and as they ate it they climbed the sand dunes and looked about them.

"There, that must be Notre Dame de Tronoën over there," said Daddy pointing to a little chapel that stood on the rising ground to their left.

"What a lot of churches and chapels you can see from here," remarked Mummy, looking round over the flat countryside which was dominated by distant towers and steeples. "There's no danger of getting lost in this part of the country as long as one can recognize the shapes of the different churches."

"And there's the lighthouse," said Robin, pointing it out. "That's another landmark."

"And the sea helps, too," put in Lucinda. "You can always hear where it is even if you can't see it."

They couldn't see it now, for the low line of the dunes hid it from view as they made their way along a sandy track toward the chapel. There were even more flowers here than there were on the dunes round the cottage, and they kept stopping to look at new varieties. They found wild thyme and sea pinks, sea holly and tall horned poppies with gleaming yellow petals, and here and there lovely sheets of silverweed spread out among the colored flowers like tiny winter gardens silvered by the frost. It was a strangely peaceful spot, filled with the scent of flowers and the sound of the sea, and dominated by the beautiful little chapel which stood on the hill with the blue sky shining through the delicate openwork of its spire. Lucinda felt she had never been quite so happy in all her life before.

As they went up the hill toward the chapel she wandered off among the flowers. Even here, as they turned away from the shore, there were clumps of sea holly, some of it covered with soft blue flowers and crisply spiked blue leaves, and some of it worn to silver lace by the salt sea winds.

Suddenly she noticed the gray ridge of a pointed roof below her. It appeared to be built into the side of the hillock on which she was standing. It seemed a strange place for a building and she went down the bank to investigate. What she found was a little holy well with a small stone shelter very much like the one at Saint-Tugen. She scrambled down and peeped inside, and sure enough there was a little figure of a woman very simply carved in soft gray stone. She wore a strange tall cap and a long full-skirted dress, and although her hands had been broken away it was easy to see that they had once been folded. Under the shelf on which she stood was the clear deep water of the holy well which overflowed into a square pool surrounded by a gray stone wall. Lucinda was so thrilled by her discovery that she forgot everything else. She never heard the others calling her, nor remembered their existence until they came down the bank in search of her.

77

"What have you found?" called Robin running ahead. "Oh, great! What a find!"

"It's a holy well like Saint Tugen's, and I found it all myself!" she said proudly.

"Oh, darling child, how lovely!" exclaimed Mummy coming down to join them. "That little figure must be very old, probably several hundred years, and how serene she is, standing there with that dreaming look on her face."

"I suppose the local women do their laundry here in this pool," observed Daddy, pointing to the walled enclosure.

"It must be wondeful to do one's washing in a holy well," said Mummy dreamily. "I'd love to look up and see that tranquil little figure gazing out over the water while I worked."

Lucinda was thrilled to find them all so interested in her discovery.

"I think she's even more exciting than Saint Tugen—I wonder why?" she said in a puzzled voice.

"I can tell you why," said Daddy. "It's because you have discovered her entirely by yourself. You didn't read about her in a guidebook or see a picture of her, but found her quite by chance and so she's your very own discovery."

At this moment a woman came toward them wheeling a barrow of washing down to the well. Daddy asked her the name of the little figure, for they had supposed her to be one of the local saints.

The woman seemed surprised that anyone should ask and replied with a little shrug that it was Notre Dame de Tronoën.

"So it's Our Lady herself," mused Daddy. "Somehow I never

thought of that, I suppose on account of that queer tall cap she's wearing."

"Perhaps the carver was a local man and copied the style of cap worn by the local women," suggested Mummy.

But now it was time to go on, so with a last lingering smile at her own special discovery Lucinda hurried after the others up the bank toward the little chapel. They went round to the far side and there they found M. Jacques with his easel set up on the grass, and on the green in front of him stood the Calvary.

"Oh how wonderful!" breathed Mummy. "I never dreamed we should find it standing here in such solitude. The surroundings must look much as they did when the Calvary was first put up nearly five hundred years ago."

For apart from the chapel and a cottage or two, the place was isolated, surrounded by little fields and quiet flat country, while below, to the west, lay the dunes and the open sea.

The Calvary stood four-square to the winds, mottled and marked by the weather and worn by the gales and salt-laden winds that swept in winter and summer over the wild Atlantic.

High in the center stood the three crosses, the scene of the Crucifixion, and below there were groups of carved stone figures showing scenes from the life of Christ. And although these were old and weatherworn they were still full of life and character. The family moved slowly from one group to the next, picking out each in turn. There was the Angel Gabriel appearing to the Virgin Mary, and then Mary visiting her cousin Elizabeth. There was the stable scene and the three wise men, the Presentation in the temple and many more. Lucinda lingered in front of the stable scene where the ox and the ass knelt with bowed heads behind Joseph.

"That ox looks just very surprised," she remarked, "but the donkey is so happy he's smiling—look you can even see his teeth!" And she reached up and stroked him very gently.

Before long M. Jacques began to pack up his things.

"Have I just got time to go back to the well and say good-by to Notre Dame?" begged Lucinda.

"Yes, if you don't stay long," said Mummy.

Lucinda raced away, round the chapel and through the grass, skipping over the blue sea holly and dodging the tall yellow ragwort as she ran. The woman had finished her washing and gone, leaving the water cloudily blue behind her. But the well itself was crystal clear and she looked down into the still depths where strands of green waterweed grew.

The late afternoon sunlight shone full into the little shelter, touching the small gray figure with golden light and warming the smooth stone folds of her flowing gown. Lucinda leaned over the water and touched her very lightly.

"Good-by," she whispered softly. "Good-by, Notre Dame, and thank you, thank you for letting me find you!"

For a moment longer she stood there, listening to the sound of the sea and the hush of the wind in the grass. And in that moment she knew she would always remember the wonderful peace of this place and the strange sweet calm of the small gray figure, standing today as she had stood through the centuries, gazing out over the dunes toward the sea.

Chapter Ten

Lucinda woke early again next morning, but this time it wasn't the kitten that woke her. It was another familiar sound—the tukka-tukka-tukka of fishing boats leaving the harbor. She jumped out of bed and ran to the window and looked out. The dawn was not far off, and it was already light enough to see the far horizon where the sea and the sky met. The lighthouse was flashing still but its beam looked pale and meaningless against the brightening sky. The harbor itself was ablaze with lights as the boats prepared to leave, while over the water like scattered stars crept the lights of those already on their way.

Maybe one of them is *Saint Corentin*, thought Lucinda, and she blew a kiss out of the window just in case. She stood leaning on the window sill until the dawn wind sent her shivering back to her warm bed, where she lay watching the feeble beam of the lighthouse flicker across her ceiling. Then her mind returned to the fishing boats setting out like a fleet of morning stars over the dawn-gray sea.

When next she awoke it was daylight. But it proved to be a disappointing day with low cloud and the feel of rain in the air.

"Not much of a day for swimming or painting either," remarked Daddy as they sat down to breakfast. "And it doesn't look to me as though it will lift in a hurry. So how would you all like to go to Quimper for the day?"

"Oh, do let's!" they chorused eagerly.

"Well then, we've just got time to catch the bus if we hurry —and that means you Lucinda, no time for dreaming now." For already her breakfast was forgotten as she sat in a trance, trying to imagine what Quimper would be like.

Mummy insisted on thick shoes and raincoats. Lucinda's laces were tangled in terrible knots and Robin's socks were lost, but somehow or other they managed to get out and catch the bus and were soon rattling on their way.

By the time they arrived in Quimper the day looked more threatening than ever, although it still was not actually raining.

"I think we'd better go and see King Gradlon first of all,"

83

said Daddy hurrying toward the Cathedral. "It wouldn't be much fun up there in one of those spires in the rain."

"Oh, Daddy, will we be able to get right up close to him?" panted Lucinda, running to keep pace with her father as he strode along.

"We certainly will. And there he is!"

They arrived in the square in front of the

Cathedral, and looking up where Daddy pointed, they saw a little figure on horseback high against the sky between the two great spires.

"Only you'll find he's not so small when you get up there. He's a long way up," said Daddy.

The space in front of the Cathedral was crowded with market stalls and around them were many peasants from the surrounding countryside wearing the costumes of their different districts. There were old men in embroidered velvet waistcoats and black velvet hats adorned with ribbons or silver buckles, and there were women in every variety of coif.

"Just look at those two," said Mummy, pointing to an elderly couple standing ·nearby. One wore the tiny Quimper coif tied under her chin with delicate crochet ribbons while the other was from Pont Aven and wore an elaborate coif of starched white lace pinned up into curving wings which nodded as she talked. At the back, pink ribbons hung over her wonderful great collar, the stiff lace standing up over her shoulders and dipping behind in a curve of tiny pleats. Beyond her another, younger woman wore a simpler coif tied on top in an upstanding bow of lace.

"Oh, and just look at that flat one over there!" cried Mummy. "I never saw such lace! But there are new ones wherever you look. I think I'll stay here and study them while you go up the tower. Then I'll meet you in the Cathedral when you come down."

Daddy led the way to the great cathedral porch decorated with saints and angels. Here they found an old woman watching over a stall of post cards. When Daddy asked her the way to

85

the tower she left her stall and opened a door in the darkest corner of the porch, showing them a flight of spiral stairs. Then without a word she went back to her cards, leaving them to find their way up alone.

As they climbed the stairs they got glimpses of the city through narrow cobwebby windows, and once they found themselves looking down inside the Cathedral itself through a barred doorway. On they went, round and round and up and up until their legs began to ache.

"Well! What are we coming to now?" exclaimed Daddy. "It looks like the darkest secret passage in the world. But since there's nowhere else to go I suppose it must be the way." He shuffled along the narrow passage, cautiously sliding his feet and feeling along the wall in the dark. Lucinda was thankful to have his hand to cling to, and if the truth were told Robin was equally thankful to have her other hand to cling to himself.

At the end of the passage there were more stairs and on they went, up and up again. Gradually it grew lighter until suddenly they stepped out into the daylight and felt the cool wind all about them, blowing through the open stonework of the spire.

And there on the roof quite close to them was King Gradlon himself, sitting on a fine stone horse with a wavy tail. The king was gazing out over the city, but the horse's head was bent as though to watch all that went on in the square below. Perhaps he could even see Mummy down there among the market stalls!

"King Gradlon looks kind of sad," observed Robin. "Maybe he's thinking about Ahès."

"Would that be the horse that saved him?" asked Lucinda,

and when Daddy nodded she went on, "he looks like a good swimmer doesn't he?"

"You ought to know!" smiled Daddy. "After all, you've become a good swimmer yourself."

At this moment they were all startled by a tremendous clanging, and for the first time they noticed two great bells on the roof behind King Gradlon.

"Must be striking the half-hour," remarked Daddy looking at his watch. "We'd better be on our way down and find Mummy."

The spiral stairs were difficult to go down.

"Makes you feel as if you're going to run away!" laughed Robin. But Daddy went ahead so that no one could run away, and they soon reached the bottom. Mummy was waiting for them in the porch.

"You must all come in and see the Cathedral. It's beautiful," she told them. "And I've found a statue of Saint Corentin that will interest you two. He's got the most realistic fish—it really looks quite wet!" And so it did. The two children could hardly bear to leave it. Lucinda looked up at the saint himself in his magnificent robes, remembering the miracle by the forest pool.

"And to think our little green ship is named for him, just the same as this huge cathedral!" she mused.

When they came out into the square it was darker then ever.

"Never mind," said Daddy. "We'll go and have something to eat and perhaps it will be better by the time we come out."

But when they came out again it was worse, not better, and a gusty wind was blowing up and beginning to sweep around the corners, snatching at people's clothes and whisking off their hats.

"Shall we visit one of the potteries?" suggested Mummy. "They are only just across the river. I noticed them as we passed in the bus."

This seemed a good idea, so they crossed one of the many bridges over the river which looked strangely dark in spite of the bright geraniums reflected in the water.

When they reached the potteries there was no one about, but there were arrows showing them the way to go. Over the door was a notice asking them not to speak to the workers.

"Why not?" asked Lucinda.

"Because it's tricky work and if they stopped to answer questions they might spoil what they were making," answered Daddy.

The arrows guided them up the stairs and through one great workroom after another. The whole place was filled with the steady throb of machinery, but otherwise there was silence. Nobody spoke and no one even looked at them as they followed the arrows round dark mysterious corners and past shelves piled high with dim gray pottery.

"Just like a sort of treasure hunt," Robin whispered to Lucinda. It was the sort of place that made you want to whisper. There was something mysterious about it all, Lucinda thought, and she kept very close to Daddy, for you never knew what you might find around the next corner; it might be a silent figure shaping a jug on a spinning potter's wheel, or it might be someone cutting away at a half-made pottery figure. It seemed a strange sort of ghostly world where the only sound was the rhythm of the machinery and the only color was gray. For everything was powdered with fine gray dust that lay so thickly on the floors that even the workers' wooden clogs were muffled into silence.

They climbed the last flight of stairs and went into the last room of all. As the door closed behind them it shut out the noise of the machinery and they seemed to have stepped into a completely different world. Here all was light and color, for this was the room in which the pottery was painted. At the long benches sat men and women, each with his own array of paints, lovely brilliant colors in shallow bowls, each with its matching brush laid across the top. Robin and Lucinda stood watching enviously, wishing that they might sit down at one of the benches and dip the brushes into those shining liquid paints. But as they watched they knew they could never paint such patterns as were appearing on the plates and bowls in front of them. There were gay little peasant figures and brilliant flowers and roosters with many-colored tails. At one bench a girl was coloring little pottery fish which would later have steel blades fixed into their open mouths and so become knives with fish-shaped handles. But there seemed no end to the wonders of this room, and they were sorry when the last arrow led them out into the street again.

In the little world of the potteries they had forgotten the larger world outside and were quite startled to step into a raging wind and feel the first drops of rain on their faces.

"Better get back across the river before it gets any worse," advised Daddy, and taking Lucinda's hand he hurried her over the wind-swept bridge.

89

When they got back to the cathedral square they found most of the market already gone, and the last stall-holders busy dismantling their stalls, some struggling with flapping canvas while others stuffed their goods into boxes before the rain could spoil them.

Daddy consulted the timetable.

"The bus won't be leaving yet awhile," he said. "Who'd like some *crêpes* before we go back?"

It turned out that everybody would, and they hurried off in search of a *crêperie*. And although many others were crowding in to escape the rain they were lucky in finding a vacant table for four.

"Oh do look!" cried Lucinda, when their *crêpes* arrived. "These plates must have come from the pottery, I saw a man painting this exact same pattern on a jug."

Somehow or other this seemed to make the *crêpes* taste better than ever. They drank out of pottery too; Mummy had coffee in a blue and white bowl with a handle at each side, and Daddy had cider in a tall mug on which was a peasant girl in a pink striped dress and yellow apron. The children had *Pscttitt* in cream-colored mugs decorated with enormous roosters perched on tiny gates.

When it was time to go for the bus it was raining hard, and they ducked their heads against it and ran all the way back to the square. In spite of the rain Lucinda managed to look up for one quick minute. She was just able to make out the dim gray shape of King Gradlon against the dim gray sky, and she even imagined she could see his horse looking straight at her, although it was hard to be sure about this with the rain in her eyes.

But now Mummy was calling. "Come along, Lucinda. Hurry, dear, the bus is here."

She and Robin found seats at the back, side by side but facing in different directions, one forward and one back. They thought this very funny.

They could scarcely see out of the windows going home because the rain slashed against the glass, running down it in streams. But there was plenty to interest them inside the bus itself. The country people crowded in with baskets and string bags stuffed full of the things they had bought in the town.

"Now isn't that a good idea?" remarked Mummy as two young women got in with neat plastic bags fitting perfectly over their tall lace coifs and kept in place with pins.

What with the noise of the rain on the roof and windows, and the chatter of French and Breton all around them, no one realized how much the wind had risen until they reached their destination. When they got out of the bus, Lucinda was almost lifted off her feet by the gale. It was impossible to speak above the roar of the wind, so they all joined hands and struggled back to the cottage as fast as they could go, beating against the wet blown sand which stung Lucinda's legs until they tingled.

But when they opend the door they found the cottage empty. The fire was alight and their meal laid ready, and leaning against the coffee jug was a note from Madame saying that she had gone to the harbor.

"But of course—the fishing boats! Oh, how worried she must be!" exclaimed Mummy anxiously.

91

Robin darted toward the door.

"I must go to the harbor too!" he declared.

"Oh no, dear, not in this storm!" cried Mummy.

As she spoke the door opened again and Madame herself walked in. They guessed at once from her pale face that the *Saint Corentin* had not returned.

"Ah, you are back—I came to see to your supper," she began.

"Now don't you give that a thought," said Mummy quickly. "I'll see to supper."

"Oh, how very good of you," said Madame gratefully. "Then I'll go back to the harbor right away. Most of the other boats are back now and all have had a bad time, the gale blew up so unexpectedly."

"I want to go to the harbor with you," said Robin going across to her side.

"No, not that," said Madame very firmly. "Your mother left you in my care and I'll not have you out on an evening like this. And anyway," she added, looking at him earnestly, "it will be far more help to me to know that you at least are safe."

"Here's a bowl of hot coffee before you go out, sit down by the fire and drink it, it will do you good," said Mummy gently, guiding Madame to a chair by the fire.

Daddy put a hand on Robin's shoulder.

"Look here," he said, "if you go to bed as usual after supper I'll promise faithfully to wake you the minute they return. How's that?"

"Will you wake me if there's any news even?" asked Robin.

"I will," promised Daddy.

"And will you wake me too?" put in Lucinda.

"Ah now, that's quite different. I'm not making any such promise to you," said Daddy. "But I think probably you'll hear them come in and wake up anyway."

Lucinda sighed, for she knew she would have to be content with this.

On her way to bed she stood for a moment with her face pressed against her rain-washed window, watching the color ebb out of the day and remembering those lighted ships setting out like stars in the morning. And now one of them, the most important of them all, had not come back.

Suddenly the lighthouse woke to life and the first beam of the evening swept across the sky. A moment later an answering flash winked out from another lighthouse far away, and soon a third opened a bright green eye in the darkness, while a ruby light glowed from the reef offshore.

"Surely with all these lights to guide them they'll be able to find their way home," she said to herself. And with this comforting thought she got into bed and was soon asleep.

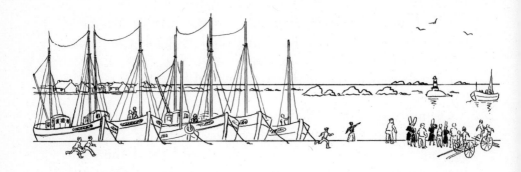

Chapter Eleven

Robin stood at his window too before he went to bed. But he was older than Lucinda and he knew that more than lights would be needed now to bring *Saint Corentin* to port. He got into bed at last, but only to toss and mutter all night long in a fitful broken sleep.

Just before dawn he crept downstairs to find Lucinda's parents sitting by the fire.

"Haven't you been to bed at all?" he asked.

"No," said Daddy with a sigh. "There's no news yet, although I've been down to the harbor several times during the night."

"Are the other boats in?" asked Robin.

"Yes, everyone else was in before midnight, but not one of them had any news of the *Saint Corentin*. She was last seen heading toward the fishing grounds quite a way down the coast."

"Well, I may as well get breakfast I suppose," said Mummy,

standing up. "Have you heard any sound of Lucinda moving yet?"

"No," said Robin, "not yet. Shall I call her as I go up?"

"Yes, dear, do," said Mummy stirring up the fire.

Breakfast was a silent meal and as soon as it was over Daddy got up.

"I'm going round to the harbor now," he said. "You two can come if you like."

"I'll stay here in case there's any message," said Mummy. "They may have put in somewhere for shelter and might send a telegram."

The worst of the storm had blown itself out and the sun was shining feebly. But the sea was wild and flecked with yellow foam and floating seaweed, and as they walked round the bay they could see great waves pouring over the sea wall on the far side of the harbor. They met an old fisherman who shook his head when he saw them and told them there was still no news of the *Saint Corentin*.

The harbor was crowded with fishermen and villagers standing about in aimless groups. There were children too, not sculling about in boats today but standing around on the quayside as silently as their elders. At the very end of the quay stood a little group of women and old men gazing out to sea. They were the parents, wives and sweethearts of the missing crew. Daddy and the two children joined them silently.

Before long Robin noticed several of the two-wheeled fish carts standing nearby, and he scrambled up on one of these to get a better view. And so it was he who first saw a glimpse of emerald green among the far gray waves.

"I . . . I think maybe she's coming!" he faltered, not daring yet to be sure. In an instant the other carts were crowded with as many as could manage to scramble on to them, and soon it was clear beyond any doubt that the little green boat was indeed coming in, struggling slowly past the lighthouse and wallowing through the surf beyond the reef. Now she rounded the last of the rocks and headed in to the harbor. Everyone stood on tip-toe, counting and counting again.

"They're all there—everyone's safe, thank God!" cried Daddy, as a great sigh of thankfulness swept through the crowd.

As the little boat came nearer they saw that she was in a very battered condition. Her foremast was broken off short and part of the wheelhouse swept away, while the deck itself was hidden under a mass of tangled nets and ropes. And worst of all—the small carved figure of Saint Corentin had vanished, although the splintered remains of his wooden frame still hung crookedly under the central window. But the men on board were smiling, although gray-faced with weariness, and Pierre shouted a cheery greeting to his mother.

When they came alongside there was a rush to seize the ropes and make them fast, and many hands stretched out to help the men ashore. There were plenty of fishermen on the quay and many of these jumped on board as the crew came off. They started at once to shift the tangled nets and sort out what they could, urging Michel and his crew to go home and get food and rest before attempting any work themselves.

So each man was claimed by his family and they moved away from the harbor in little groups. The two elder le Roux boys were married, and after talking awhile with their parents they went toward the village with their wives, while the family from the sand dunes turned toward the shore. Madame walked between Michel and Pierre with Daddy and the children following behind. They all walked in silence. The only sound came from the sea thundering in on the rocks below.

When they got back to the cottage the green door flew open and they saw that Mummy had stoked the fire to a roaring blaze and had food and steaming coffee ready on the table.

It was some time before the whole story came out, but at last, when they were thoroughly warmed and fed, Michel began to tell it, quietly at first, then his voice growing more and more excited as the tale went on. He forgot about Lucinda and told it in French, and so she only learned later how the engine had failed just as the first of the storm hit them on the edge of the exposed fishing grounds. As his voice rose and fell Lucinda leaned on the arm of his chair, trying to guess at the story of the helpless boat's struggle against the storm as the wind drove her toward the rocks. Suddenly Michel became aware of the child's tense face so close to his own.

"*Hélas!*" he cried, slipping his arm around her. "I'm forget-

97

ting you speak no French. From here I will go on in English. And anyway the best part, the happy part, is coming," he said as Lucinda relaxed against him with a smile.

"Now," he explained, "here we are with no engine, driving in toward the rocks, and the daylight going. The great lighthouse wakes and tries to beckon us home, but how can we go with no engine? We try to rig a sail but the mast snaps immediately, and then a great wave sweeps over the boat taking part of the wheelhouse with it and our own dear image of Saint Corentin too."

Lucinda pressed against him, holding her breath.

"But now comes the miracle." He smiled. "Just when it seems that nothing can save us there comes a brilliant flash of lightning—"

"I saw it!" interrupted Robin excitedly. "I woke up in the night and it lit up my whole room."

"It did more than that," went on Michel. "It lit up all the land beyond the reef, and in the instant of its flash I saw low sand dunes just like our own dunes here, and among them the small bell-tower of some tiny church or chapel. And in that second of time I prayed to God and the saint of that little chapel, whoever he might be, to save us from the rocks."

He paused a moment, staring thoughtfully into the fire, and then went on very quietly, "And in the minutes that followed my prayer was answered; the wind shifted a point, two points, and within less than half an hour it was blowing us steadily away from the reef. And more than that—before the hour was up we got the engine going and were able to start for home."

Nobody spoke, but everyone relaxed and a sigh of relief went up from the group around the table.

"And I'll tell you something," he went on, looking from one face to another. "I vowed a vow right there and then to find that little chapel in the dunes and go there with all my crew to give thanks for our deliverance. And when I told my plan to the others, Pierre and the men made a vow of their own. Tell them about it, Pierre, my boy."

But when they turned to Pierre they saw that he was fast asleep with his head on the kitchen table.

"Ah, poor boy, he's worn out and no wonder," exclaimed Madame. "Come now, away to your beds the pair of you." She roused Pierre gently and helped him to his feet, and he stumbled away on her arm, no more than half awake.

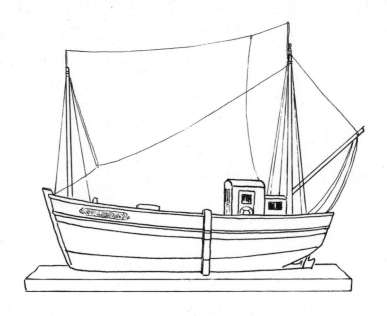

Chapter Twelve

When Pierre woke later in the day he almost stumbled over the two children sitting silently outside his door waiting for him to come out.

"Please, Pierre, tell us about your vow," they begged as soon as he appeared.

"Come out into the sunshine then," said Pierre, leading the way to the long bench under the fig tree. "Well now, it's this. We've vowed to make a model boat like they used to make in the old days, and present it to the chapel in the dunes—it's one of the old customs of our country to make a model boat as a thank offering when one has been saved from shipwreck. So we're all going to make it together. But now I must go to the harbor. My father's gone already I see, and they may be needing me."

"We'll come, too," said Robin.

They found the rest of the crew already assembled with many helpers and hard at work on the poor battered *Saint Corentin*.

There was a great deal to be done. The shattered mast would have to be replaced and much of the rigging renewed, and a new door must be made for the wheelhouse and new boarding fixed around it. The only thing that could never be replaced was the little old wooden saint that the waves had swept away.

But the worst trouble of all was the faulty engine, as examination showed that it would need a new part which could not be provided locally. It would have to be sent by rail and that would mean a long delay. So it looked as though the boat would not be ready to put to sea for a week or ten days at the least.

However, everyone set to work to do all that could be done as speedily as possible. As soon as Pierre could be spared from more urgent jobs he got permission to build a bench in a corner of one of the harbor sheds, and here he collected tools and wood and string and glue and everything else he would need for making the model.

Late that evening, when work for the day was finished, the crew collected in the shed and work began on the model. In the days that followed it took shape rapidly—when any one of the crew found himself with a spare moment during the day he would hurry to the bench and put in ten minutes or so on the model. It was a piecemeal way of doing things, but because everyone was keen on the job it worked suprisingly well. There was always someone or other busy at the workbench and Lucinda and Robin spent much of the day leaning against it, watching the work with breathless interest. And although these were anxious days for Michel and his crew it was a happy time for the children who learned to know the men as never before. And best of all they had Pierre with them all day long.

It was several days before Michel could spare time from the work on the boat to go and look for the chapel, although the thought of it was constantly in his mind. But at last one morning, right after breakfast, he spread out his charts on the kitchen table.

"What's a chart?" asked Lucinda, coming over to stare at the unfamiliar picture.

"Like a map, only of sea instead of land," explained Robin. "All this is the sea and this little bit is land, and these things are reefs or rocks, and here's a lighthouse, and I think this must be a bell buoy over here."

"Now we were here, somewhere between this lighthouse and the reef," mused Michel bending over the chart. "So the little chapel must be somewhere in this region—it was only such a tiny place that I doubt they'd mark it at all. But now I see where it must be, I think I'll go over there and look for it today."

"I suppose Lucinda and I couldn't go too and help you look?" asked Robin.

"Why, yes, of course, come along if you want to," said

Michel. "But you'll have to be ready to catch the bus in half an hour."

When Madame heard what they were planning she called to Robin.

"Robin, run along to the village, there's a good lad. I haven't enough cheese for the three of you." She gave him money and told him to choose whatever cheese he liked.

"Are we going to have a picnic, just Robin and me and Michel?" asked Lucinda eagerly as Robin hurried off.

"Yes," said Madame. "It'll take you quite a while to get there and back and find the chapel as well."

At this moment Daddy called to Lucinda.

"Here's money for your bus fare and Robin's, too," he said. "Be careful not to lose it and be sure not to be a nuisance to Michel."

Suddenly Madame called from the kitchen.

"Robin, Robin."

"He's gone," said Lucinda.

"Ah, there now—and I forgot to tell him to get bread, and there's so little time," said Madame in a flurried voice.

"Couldn't I get it?" said Lucinda. "I often shop for Mummy at home."

"Ah, but at home you shop in English," smiled Madame. "However, I don't see why you shouldn't try here all the same— that is if your Daddy agrees."

"Fine—good idea." said Daddy.

"Well then, listen carefully," said Madame. "You go down that road over there, 'Rue de la Mer' it's called."

"Does that mean 'Road of the Sea'?" interrupted Lucinda.

"That's right," said Madame. "Now then, the first shop you'll come to on your left is the *Pharmacie*, and next door to that is the *Boulangerie* which is the shop you want. It has the word '*Boulangerie*' over the door in big letters, and the window will be full of bread, if it hasn't all been sold. Go in and ask for '*trois petits pains*,' that means three little breads. You would call them rolls at home only your rolls are smaller. Now do you think you can remember that?"

"Yes, yes easily!" cried Lucinda, hopping on one leg in her impatience to be off.

"The *petits pains* will be ten francs each, so there you are, there are thirty francs."

Lucinda hurried off and soon came to the *Rue de la Mer*, and almost at once there was the *Pharmacie* with a window full of shampoos and soaps, just as it would be at home. And there next door was the *Boulangerie*. She thought she would have been able to find it by the smell of fresh bread alone even if its name hadn't been over the door.

There were several people there before her and she stood looking about her at the wonderful loaves of bread—round rings of bread that she could have worn on her arms like giant bracelets, and extraordinary long thin loaves standing on end in a special basket.

Now it was her turn and she stepped forward hoping the shopkeeper would think she was really French.

"*Trois petits pains, s'il vous plaît*," she said clearly, handing over her money. The shopkeeper understood her perfectly, and the next minute there she was, walking up the *Rue de la Mer* with three warm *petits pains* in her hands like any French girl.

The bus ride did not take long, and when they got out they found themselves in a tiny village straggling along a sandy shore. A number of bright small boats lay on their sides on the sand, stranded by the ebbing tide, and beyond them a line of strangely shaped rocks stretched along the shore. Beyond again was the blue sea, scattered with jagged reefs and among them a little lighthouse on a rock.

"It does look an awfully dangerous place for a boat like *Saint Corentin*," said Robin looking out at the rock-strewn bay.

Michel walked out across the sand and stood at the very edge of the sea looking back toward the shore.

"Now," he said, pointing inland, "I think it must be some-where just about there." He strode away so fast that the children had to run to keep pace with him. At the top of the dunes he paused and looked about again. There were several houses in sight but no chapel to be seen. They walked along the top of the dunes in silence until suddenly Michel startled them both with a tremendous shout of "*Voilà!*" pointing excitedly at a small gray bell-tower beyond a hedge.

They hurried toward it, crossing a green buttercup meadow through which ran a shallow stream, and presently they reached the little chapel. It was so low that it seemed to have sunk into the ground with the years, and so old that its worn stones were coated with golden lichen. Inside it was plainly whitewashed, but on one wall Lucinda saw the Virgin and Child in shallow relief on the stone. To enter the chapel they went down two steps which made the place seem more sunken than ever. The floor was of smooth hard earth.

"Oh, they've got a ship already!" exclaimed Lucinda pointing at a small three-masted schooner which hung from one of the rafters.

"That won't matter at all—some chapels have three or four, or even more if they're lucky. I've no doubt they'll be delighted to have another one here."

The next thing to be done was to go and find the priest, but Michel decided they would have their picnic first. They chose a flat rock on the shore and sat there facing the sea. Lucinda thought her *petit pain* the nicest part of the meal, and Robin thought the same of the cheese he had bought in the village.

Michel sat for a while looking thoughtfully out across the sea where he had so nearly lost his life, and he murmured to himself, "*Protégez-moi, Seigneur, ma barque est si petite et la mer est si grande.*"

"What does that mean?" asked Lucinda.

"It's an old Breton prayer," explained Robin. "It means 'Protect me, Lord, my boat is so small and the sea so big.'"

Chapter Thirteen

Lucinda and Robin were left to amuse themselves on the beach while Michel went in search of the priest. It was an exciting coastline with several little cottages right on the shore, their boats drawn up in front of their doors.

"Musn't it be just wonderful to live in a place like this?" remarked Robin, looking enviously at two small boys hauling their flat-bottomed boat up the beach.

Lucinda was busy picking up shells as she went along.

"Just look at these," she said. "I've got all the colors of the fishermen's clothes in shells—mussels for the blue ones and these others for the browns and pinks, and these little yellow ones for the oilskins." She spread them out on a flat-topped rock as she spoke.

"Let's go and look at those queer rocks over there," suggested Robin. They were very queer rocks indeed, very big and so fantastic in shape that Lucinda decided they were just a little frightening. They wandered slowly from rock to rock, stopping to poke in the sea-weedy pools between them.

"Look here! There are all sorts of things in this one," said Robin, crouched down over a deep dark pool.

But Lucinda was looking up, not down, and she gave such a sudden shout that Robin jumped up thinking she must have hurt herself.

"Look, Robin, it's Saint Corentin!" she cried, pointing to a deep crevice in the rocks.

"Saint Corentin—what do you mean?"

"In there among the seaweed, it's him, I *know* it is, I can even see his fish. But why is he here, is it a shrine or what?"

At first Robin didn't answer, he was too surprised.

"A shrine? Of course it isn't—this is our own Saint Corentin, the one that was washed off the ship. But we'll have to get him quickly," he added as a wave swept round the rock on which they stood. "The tide has turned and it's coming in fast. Look, you go back and stand over there while I get him out."

But it wasn't so easy to get him out because for several days the waves had been washing him into the crevice more firmly with every tide.

"Oh do be careful, Robin!" warned Lucinda as a wave washed over his feet. But Robin paid no attention, struggling frantically to loosen the little figure.

"It's moving!" he panted. "Only the bottom part's wedged now."

The next wave swept over his knees but still he went on struggling, and he was wet to the waist when he finally staggered backwards triumphantly with Saint Corentin in his arms. He waded back to Lucinda whose own feet were already wet, and they ran up the shore out of reach of the waves before stopping to examine the little figure.

"He's hardly been damaged at all," marveled Robin studying him carefully. "Even his crook isn't broken. You know it's a good thing Michel's father wasn't too good a carver. If he'd made this crook as thin as it ought to be it would have been broken now for sure."

"What about your clothes?" asked Lucinda anxiously. "You're awfully wet you know."

"Who cares? They'll dry in all this wind and sun. Oh, Lucinda, just think how thrilled Michel will be—and there he is—" He broke into a run and raced up the dunes with Lucinda hurrying after him.

"Hello, Hello!" called Michel as he saw them coming. "Well, I found the priest and he . . . but . . . but Robin what have you got there? Let me see . . . it is . . . it is . . . it's Saint Corentin himself!"

Between them they told him the story all in a breathless rush while Michel turned the little figure round and round in his hands, examining it from every side as though he could hardly believe it was real.

"Marvelous," he kept saying. "Marvelous, that you should be guided to the actual rock to find him like that—and to think he's been there washed by every tide this week! We must carry him in the procession too, I feel sure the priest will agree. I would like to feel he has been blessed before we return him to his niche under the wheelhouse window."

"Was he pleased to hear about Pierre's boat?" asked Robin.

"Indeed he was, and he tells me that the *Pardon* of this little chapel is to be celebrated on the Sunday after next. And he says that if we come on that day our model boat will be carried in the procession for the Benediction of the Sea. We must get home and tell the others so that they may be sure to get it ready in time."

"What's a *Pardon*?" asked Lucinda.

"Ah now, a *Pardon* is something I believe you will find nowhere else but in *Bretagne*—Brittany that is. It is the *fête* of the patron saint of a church or chapel or sometimes even a holy well —these *Pardons* occur all over Brittany on the same days every year. So it is a particularly fortunate chance that the *Pardon* here should be going to take place at this particular time. But now come along, we must get our bus home and tell the news to the others."

Nothing was said about Robin's wet clothes or Lucinda's sandals. Michel was far too occupied with Saint Corentin to notice anything else. And they were dry anyway by the time they got home.

It seemed as though the finding of Saint Corentin inspired

every one of the crew and the work went ahead faster than ever on the two boats, the real one and the model. At last the real one was finished, all except the engine part for which they were still waiting.

"We'll give her a new coat of paint while we wait," announced Michel.

"You'll paint her the same colors as before, won't you?" asked Lucinda anxiously. "I think she's the prettiest boat in the harbor as she is."

"Indeed I will," he said, smiling down at her. "I think she's the prettiest one myself."

Even Lucinda and Robin were allowed to give a hand with the painting, working at some of the less important parts with two shades of green. And when this was done the model was painted also in two shades of green exactly like the original. She even had the thin red line between the two colors.

"And as soon as she's dry we'll add her name and number," said Pierre.

One of the crew made a pair of tiny lifebelts and these were now fixed on either side of the little wheelhouse. And then Michel surprised them all by producing a tiny copy of Saint Corentin.

"Although I'm afraid I'm no more of a hand at carving than my father was!" he said apologetically.

"Oh, I think he's simply lovely, just as nice as the real one," said Lucinda, fingering the roughly-cut little figure very gently.

It was decided that Robin should be allowed to carry the real Saint Corentin in the procession, as he was the one who had rescued him, and he was to travel to the chapel with the rest of the crew early on the morning of the *Pardon*. Lucinda and her parents would follow in the bus with Madame later in the day.

Lucinda tried not to be envious as she peeped out of her bedroom window and saw them start off in the early morning before it was really light.

But Madame seemed to guess how she felt, for she called her upstairs after breakfast. She had an old-fashioned wooden box on her lap and she searched through its jumbled contents until she found what she wanted.

"There!" she said, lifting out a little silver cross on a delicate silver chain. "This was given to me when I attended my first *Pardon* as a baby, and as I have no daughter I should like you to have it, to remind you of your first *Pardon*—for I haven't forgotten that it was you who found Saint Corentin and brought us so much happiness."

As she spoke, she fastened the chain round Lucinda's neck.

"You mean . . . you mean. . . ." hesitated Lucinda, fingering the little cross. "You mean for me to keep for my very own?"

"To keep for the rest of your life, my dear, to remind you of your first *Pardon*."

"Oh!" breathed Lucinda, flinging her arms round Madame's neck. "I shall really feel *part* of the *Pardon* now!"

The chapel bell was ringing as they came toward it and they could see the white coifs of the women coming along the roads from all directions.

Three little stalls had been erected right outside the chapel and Lucinda caught a glimpse of brightly colored sweets and toys as she hurried by.

The chapel was already full when they arrived, but a woman looked up from a bench near the door and shifted her baby to make room for Lucinda. As she squeezed into the vacant space Lucinda looked at the baby and marveled at her clothes. She was all in white with a satin bonnet encrusted with silver beads, and on her hands she wore doll-sized white lace gloves with real fingers. Around her neck hung a tiny cross on a silver chain just like Lucinda's own.

As more and still more people arrived, they gathered in groups about the open door and window. The shouts of the stall-holders calling their wares penetrated the chapel, and the quiet voice of the priest was often interrupted by the laughter of children outside on the grass, and the shrill blasts of the whistles they had bought from the toy stall. But this merely made the sunlit scene outside more truly a part of the simple service.

Lucinda could not understand a single word but she felt the peace of the service flow over her as she sat on the hard wooden bench, looking up over the crowded coifs to two kind wooden saints who looked down from the walls on either side of the altar. Then her eyes turned to the little old ship hanging from the rafters above. And as she looked a light wind blew through the open window, stirring the filmy cobwebs that festooned the rigging like ghostly sails.

Presently everyone got up and streamed out into the sunshine. Lucinda thought the service was over until she saw the little procession forming outside on the grass between the booths where young seamen and girls waited with crosses and banners. Behind them stood Pierre and three others with the

new model boat on their shoulders, and beyond them she saw
Robin carrying Saint Corentin fixed to a stand like a wooden
tray. Robin was gazing straight in front of him but Lucinda
saw his cheeks grow pink and knew that he had seen her.

Then they all set off over the buttercup meadow toward the
sand dunes and the sea. Here they trooped down on to the
shore and the priests and standard-bearers went right out over
the seaweed to stand on the very edge of the tide for the Benediction of the Sea. Beyond them little boats bobbed at their

moorings, and beyond the boats wild waves dashed up over the
lighthouse on the rocks, reminding them all why they were here
today.

While an ancient priest chanted the Benediction and
sprinkled the incoming waves with holy water, a young girl
wandered among the crowd distributing leaflets on which were
typed two hymns with many verses, a French hymn on one side
of the sheet and a Breton one on the other. Soon everyone
started to sing the French hymn to a lovely haunting melody,

and as they sang they all trooped up the beach and over the dunes toward the chapel.

"The words of this hymn are lovely," murmured Mummy, translating some of the verses for Lucinda:

> "Blessed Star of the Sea
> Guide my boat to the shore,
> Guard me from all shipwreck
> White Star of the morning.
>
> One is so far and so alone
> Out there in the sea's immensity—
> So little in the silence
> Where the great waves curl."

Lucinda walked with her hand in her mother's, watching the colored banners sway against the sky. The first was gold and crimson, and showed Jesus standing in a tiny boat on the crest of a curling wave. The second was blue and white embroidered with a picture of the Virgin and Child in a boat with a white-winged angel. Behind the banners she could just see the mast of the model ship swaying above the heads of the crowd as though tossed on a stormy sea. And suddenly she remembered that they had come today to give thanks for a real ship saved from a real sea storm. And with this thought, one more "Thank You" drifted up from the heart of the *Pardon* into the sunny sky.

Chapter Fourteen

"This dark sort of light makes you feel you ought to whisper doesn't it?" said Lucinda who had never before been out so early in the morning.

They were walking over the dunes toward the harbor, she and Robin leading the way, followed by Mummy and Daddy and Madame, and they were on their way to see the *Saint Corentin* start out. It was still quite dark with only a streak of light in the eastern sky to show where the sun would rise. When they reached the beach the tide had turned and the sweeping beams of the lighthouse were reflected across the wet sand.

But when they came to the harbor they found it as bright as day, for the great arc lights were blazing overhead, shutting out the darkness that lay beyond the quay.

"Golly—it's as busy as it is when the boats come home in the evenings," remarked Robin in surprise. He found it hard to believe that all this activity went on in the early hours of every morning while he was still asleep.

The quay was crowded with fishermen hurrying to and fro, some in sabots and some in rubber boots, carrying baskets of food and crates of drink to be stowed in the waiting boats, many of which were ready to start. In the midst of them was *Saint Corentin*, her green paint gleaming under the lights, and the little old saint with his battered fish smiling calmly out from his frame.

"*Saint Corentin* will be glad to get to sea again," remarked Lucinda, listening to the eager throb of the engine and the cheerful shouts of the crew. She was surprised when Robin gave a sudden low whistle behind her.

"Well, blow me down! Just look who's here!" he exclaimed.

Lucinda spun round, and there, trotting along very jauntily with his tail straight up in the air was a small gray shadow with a white-tipped tail.

"Matelot!" she gasped.

"So he's escaped again!" said Robin. "What a cat! You know it looks as though you really are right about his wanting to stay by the sea. But come on—I see Pierre getting ready to cast off." Seizing her by the arm he dragged her through the crowd.

Everyone surged forward, slapping *Saint Corentin's* newly painted hull and reaching out to shake the hands of the crew and wish them well as the little ship cast off and slowly backed away from the quayside. As she turned in a swirl of ruffled water and headed for the open sea a cheer went up from the harbor, and in that moment the crimson rim of the rising sun appeared above the horizon. Lucinda looked toward the lighthouse and saw that it was out.

Then she remembered Matelot. But although she searched through the crowd and among the crates and baskets standing on the quay he was nowhere to be seen.

"Well, I really think we must leave him to do as he wants," said Daddy. "He seems to be a very determined little animal, and I'm beginning to think he's quite able to fend for himself."

"Anyway you can look for him this evening when we come back here to meet the boats," said Mummy, who was anxious to get the children home for breakfast.

Just as they reached the cottage the postman arrived with a parcel.

"Aha!" said Daddy. "I hoped this might come today."

"What is it?" asked Lucinda curiously.

"Something I ordered in Quimper the other day," replied Daddy. He untied the string, then handed the parcel to her to open. She pulled off the paper and out rolled a pair of red rubber frog feet exactly like Robin's. Tucked inside the toe of one of them was a pair of diving goggles.

Lucinda was too amazed to say a single word, but Robin said enough for the two of them.

"Gee—they're neat!" he cried, snatching up the goggles and

peering through them. "Just like mine only newer. And these frog feet are simply terrific! We'll be able to have races under water now, and dive for treasure and everything—oh golly, can we go and swim this morning?"

Lucinda found her voice at last although it was not much more then a whisper when it came.

"Are they really for me?" she asked, looking up at Daddy with shining eyes.

"Of course they are," he smiled. "I've always said you should have some as soon as you learned to swim."

Well of course after that there was only one way to spend the morning, and as soon as they could get ready they hurried off to the nearest sandy bay.

The frog feet weren't easy to manage at first, and Lucinda kept stopping to rest and stand with her face on the surface, peering down through the goggles at the treasures that lay on the sandy bottom. But at last, with Daddy and Robin to help her, she managed a few short dives and was finally able to grab up a handful of pebbles and shells from the bottom.

"I've got some treasure!" she spluttered, struggling to her feet and pushing her goggles up into her hair. She opened her hand to examine the shells and colored pebbles. Among them was an oblong of mother-o'-pearl.

"Why it's just like a fish!" she exclaimed, dipping it into the sea to wash off the sand. It was like a fish with a slender tail and a mark where the eye should be.

"I'll pretend he's Saint Corentin's magic fish and keep him all my life," she said.

"And now it's time to come in and get dressed," said Mummy, and seeing Lucinda hesitate she added, "and I see Madame has put *petits pains* and peaches into the picnic basket for lunch."

They returned to the harbor early in the afternoon to be sure of being in time for *Saint Corentin's* return. The quayside was quiet and deserted, but out in the harbor itself several of the local children were sculling about in their fathers' boats, their happy shouts echoing over the water. Lucinda and Robin stood watching them while Mummy and Daddy settled down on a pile of planks. They unpacked their sketching things and were soon so absorbed in their work that they did not immediately notice when the children came and stood beside them.

Robin nudged Lucinda.

"Go on," he muttered. "You ask."

Only then did Mummy look up. Lucinda took a deep breath and looked at her imploringly.

"Please, we want to do something very special today," she began. "Oh please, please do say we can."

"It all depends what it is," said Mummy warily, and her face took on that cautious look that Lucinda knew so well. She took another deep breath, then her words tumbled out in a rush.

"Well, you remember the first day we came you said you'd let me go out in a boat like those boys if only I could swim?"

"Oh, darling, I didn't quite say that," objected Mummy. "I said I *wouldn't* let you go out if you *couldn't* swim."

"Well isn't that the same?" asked Lucinda feeling rather muddled. "And anyway I really can swim now."

"And it's only just out there with the others we want to go,"

121

urged Robin. "Old Henri said we could borrow his boat, and I know how to scull. Pierre taught me."

"And we'd be awfully close where you could see us all the time," finished Lucinda.

Her parents looked at one another and Lucinda watched their faces intently.

"Well. . . ." began her father slowly.

"Oh Daddy, Daddy, I knew you'd say yes," she shouted joyfully, throwing her arms around him.

"But I haven't said yes," laughed Daddy.

"No, but you're going to, I know by your face."

"Well as a matter of fact I was going to say that I don't think you'd be likely to come to much harm as long as you stay right here where we can watch you. But first of all let's have a look at this boat of Henri's."

"It's just down here," said Robin leading the way to the nearest jetty. The boat was a small flat-bottomed one, wide and very sturdy.

"What do they call this sort of boat?" asked Daddy looking it over.

"It's a *canot*, the kind they use for landing the catches from the fishing boats," explained Robin.

"It's beautiful isn't it?" said Lucinda gazing admiringly at the stumpy little craft.

"Well it certainly looks pretty safe and solid and that's what matters to me," smiled Daddy. "But remember, you will have to keep still and do exactly as Robin tells you. Come along now, you'd better sit here." And he helped her down on to the forward seat. Robin climbed down behind her and settled his single oar into its notch in the stern, and almost before she realized what was happening they were moving. The boat swayed more than she expected as Robin swung the oar from side to side, but she grew accustomed to the motion and was able to loosen her grip on the side of the boat and spare a hand to wave to Daddy.

Pierre had taught Robin to scull very well and in a few minutes they were out in the middle of the harbor among the other children. As Lucinda listened to the chatter of French and Breton around her it seemed as unreal as a dream. It was hard to believe she was actually out here in a real boat among these children she had envied. But when she looked across to the quay Mummy waved her paintbrush, which proved that it certainly wasn't a dream. Lucinda hugged herself with happiness and decided that she must be the luckiest child in the world.

But now one of the children raised his head and listened, and soon they all heard the tukka-tukka-tukka of the first returning fishing boat. As it chugged slowly in to its mooring one of the men leaned over the side and shouted something to the children.

"What did he say?" asked Lucinda who had caught the name *Saint Corentin* in the middle of the sentence.

"He says *Saint Corentin's* got the most marvelous catch anyone's ever seen!" cried Robin excitedly. "And here she comes! Let's wait right here and meet her at her buoy. The tide's low so they'll be mooring out here this evening anyway, and coming ashore in the *canot*. And golly, just look at those gulls!" he added as the *Saint Corentin* came closer. "That shows what a lot of fish there must be on board."

As they neared the buoy Michel cut off the engine and the

boat drifted on in silence, with Pierre hanging over the side with a boathook, ready to pick up the buoy.

"We've got the biggest catch you ever saw!" he shouted exultantly. His brothers' beaming faces appeared over his shoulder as they came to the side for a moment, waving the fish they were cleaning. Above them Michel leaned out of the wheelhouse window.

"Hi, you two—don't go!" he shouted. "We'll need your help. You can take the first load of fish ashore for us and bring back any extra boxes and baskets you can lay hands on. We're going to need everything we can find to carry all this fish ashore."

Lucinda's face went white and Robin's crimson with delight, for here was Michel himself giving them a real job to do, a man-sized job that was usually done by the fishermen themselves. They caught one another's eyes and smiled triumphantly, for they felt they had really been accepted now as members of the crew.

"You'd better move right up into the bow, Lucinda, to make room," suggested Robin as the crew started to hand down the boxes. The fish were as neatly packed as sardines in a tin, and the men piled the boxes one on top of another until the boat would hold no more.

"I guess you'd better stand up once we get going with this load," advised Robin as he pushed the *canot* away from the boat's side.

"Don't forget to bring back more boxes and baskets," shouted Michel as they moved off.

For a moment Lucinda steadied herself against the pile of boxes, then, as she grew accustomed to the steady roll of the boat, she straddled her legs like the other children and stuck her hands in her pockets, and so they came in to the jetty with their load, looking for all the world like a couple of fishermen's children. Daddy and Mummy were there to meet them, together with most of the usual harbor crowd, for news of *Saint Corentin's* record catch had already spread to the village. Someone had brought a two-wheeled cart and there were many hands to help unload the *canot*, and then reload it with empty boxes.

"Come on, Lucinda, we'll have to get back. Michel is waiting for these," said Robin importantly. Lucinda skipped into her place in the bow, smelling of fish and feeling herself a real fisherman's child. She looked it too, for although she did not realize it there were several silver fish-scales in her hair.

When they got back to the *Saint Corentin* they found a fresh load of crates packed and ready to go ashore. Pierre climbed down into the *canot* between them, and as soon as the empty boxes were unloaded he stacked the full ones in their place, piling them one on top of another. The *canot* was fully loaded and ready to start when Michel looked down at them over the side.

"You two still there?" he called, "Ah—well I almost forgot to tell you that we found a stowaway on board when we got out to sea."

"A stowaway?" echoed the children. "Where did he hide?"

"Down in the cabin on one of the bunks, and we never discovered him until we were well on our way."

He bent down as he spoke and reappeared with something in his hand. It was a small gray kitten with a white-tipped tail.

"Matelot!" cried Lucinda for the second time that day. She

stood very still, gripping the edge of a fish box until it hurt, not daring to ask the question that was in her mind. But Michel seemed to guess what she was thinking, and, smiling down at her, he said, "Well, I must say this little cat is a very determined creature with a character all his own. He knows what he wants, that's certain, and he knows how to get it too. I don't really approve of cats on fishing boats as a rule—some people say they bring bad luck. But as this one's brought us the best luck we've ever known on his very first trip I guess we'll let him stay."

"Oh Michel!" said Lucinda with a grateful smile.

Pierre came to stand beside his father.

"There'll always be plenty of fish for him here," he said, holding a scrap to the kitten as he spoke, "and Mother will give me a drop of milk for him in the mornings I know."

Matelot licked the fishy taste from his whiskers, and it seemed to Lucinda that he winked at her as he did so.

"Oh I'm so glad he's found a real sea-home at last!" she said happily.

"Time we were getting this load ashore," said Robin. He turned the *canot* toward the shore as he spoke, then slipping his oar into position he called over his shoulder, "Say, Lucinda, keep an eye on those boxes will you? It's quite a load and we mustn't let it slip."

Lucinda braced herself against the pile of boxes, spreading her arms to keep them steady.

"That's fine," smiled Robin, leaning on his oar. "It sure takes two to do this job." For a moment he seemed almost as old as Pierre.

Lucinda remembered how she had seen him on the day of

her arrival helping to unload the catch on the quay, and she found it hard to believe that she was now a part of this busy scene herself.

As they moved across the harbor she looked back over the water. The *Saint Corentin* was swinging at her moorings. Pierre had already turned away and was helping to hoist the wet brown nets up to the mast to dry. But Michel still stood where they had left him with the kitten in his arms, and behind him the little old saint smiled down on the scene, clasping his silver fish.